BONES OF THE MOON

BONES OF THE MOON

Jonathan Carroll

ARBOR HOUSE | William Morrow | New York

To Phyllis Westberg.

Here is another box for you.
It is the only one I knew how to make by hand.

First published by Arbor House in 1988

Copyright © 1987 by Jonathan Carroll

Manufactured in the United States of America

Published in Canada by Fitzhenry & Whiteside, Ltd.

"At North Farm," in *A Wave* by John Ashbery.
Copright © 1981, 1982, 1983, 1984 by John Ashbery. All rights reserved.
Reprinted by permission of Viking Penguin, Inc.

Somewhere someone is travelling furiously toward you,
At incredible speed, travelling day and night,
Through blizzards and desert heat, across torrents, through
  narrow passes
But will he know where to find you,
recognize you when he sees you,
Give you the thing he has for you?
                              'At North Farm,' John Ashbery

PART ONE

1

The Axe Boy lived downstairs. We were friendly because he was forever walking an ugly little dog I patted when I bumped into them in the hall.

As you've seen from the pictures, he was nothing special to look at. The only odd thing I noticed was his eyeglasses: they were almost always dirty—that foggy, smudged look which makes you want to take out your own hanky and give them a good cleaning.

'A good boy.' Why do newspapers always use terms like that? 'Everyone who knew him thought of the murderer as a good boy who loved his parents, was a member of the Eagle Scouts and spent his spare time collecting Asian stamps.'

Even my wonderful husband Danny said that after most of the grisly details came out. 'He seemed like a good kid, didn't he, Cullen? "Axe Boy"? Jesus, what a thing to call someone!'

'Danny, our young friend "Axe Boy" Alvin Williams chopped his mother and sister into *pieces* exactly one floor below our apartment. A good boy he is *not.*'

Danny had that quality and most of the time I loved him very much for it: the world is to be forgiven. Axe Boys, dogs that shit in the middle of the sidewalk, dangerous drivers . . . they know not what they do.

I forgive nothing. If you stole my orange crayon in the fifth grade, you're still on my hit list, buster.

We were eating breakfast and Danny was reading the story to me from the paper. The thought of that murderous creep snoozing below us not long before still made my fanny tingle.

'He says he didn't know what came over him.'

3

'Oh, really? Well, I hope the next thing that comes over him is a noose!'

'Cullen, you've interrupted me four times since I began reading this article to you. Would you like me to go on, or would you rather do a monologue?'

But he smiled when he said this because he wasn't really angry. When Danny got angry, he became quiet. Then you ran and hid under the bed for a very long time until he spoke again.

'You can go on, but he doesn't deserve any sympathy.'

Danny ruffled the paper and cleared his throat. 'He said he didn't know what came over him because he loved his mother and sister very much.' He shook his head. 'My God, what would it be like if that was your kid?' He looked at me as if I had the answer. 'Whenever you see the parents of a kid like this on television, being interviewed, they always look so hurt and confused. All that time and effort they've put in over the years. The new bicycles they bought, trips to the doctor, packages from Grandma . . . So what ends up happening? Mom borrows his pen and for some reason he goes totally berserk. I wonder if it was this bad in the old days?'

'Danny, please don't start. "The old days" were probably just as bad as now; people just use them as an excuse to condemn things.'

'I'm not going to "start". It's just that whenever I read about something like this, I get all guilty. You know what I mean? Why should we be so lucky? We still love each other, the baby's great, I make good money . . .'

He shrugged and drank his coffee. There wasn't anything I could say because he was right—we *were* lucky people, and if I could do anything about it, it would stay that way for the next fifty years.

I fell in love with Danny James when it was unfashionable to fall in love with anything but causes. Spell that with a capital 'C', please. That was back in the 1970s when everybody hated the war in Vietnam and stores sold only incense and tacky Indian clothes by the million. I shouldn't be so snotty, because I wore too much patchouli perfume and carried my very own copy of *The Prophet* with me wherever I went. Thank God things change. Is there anyone around whose past doesn't make them cringe?

We met in college in New Jersey and were introduced by the girl Danny later married—Evelyn Hernuss, who was my room-mate in freshman year.

4

He was in love with her. But at the time I was in love with Jim Vanderberg, so I didn't pay much attention to Danny James. Jim and I were convinced we were destined to get married and go off to a Peace Corps posting in some ravaged section of the world, where they would desperately need us and we would go around feeling like little saints for a couple of years. But the worm turns!

Jim and I later broke up over an advanced case of apathy. And three months after their marriage in junior year, Evelyn Hernuss James died in a car crash with her mother and father on their way home from one of Danny's basketball games.

I had taken the semester off to campaign for a Presidential peace candidate and was in Chicago when I heard about her death. There was little I could do besides write Danny a letter telling him how sorry I was. Evelyn was one of the good ones—all the way down the line.

In what seemed a week, I received a thick letter back from Danny, spilling every gut he had on to the page. I wrote back and he wrote back and I wrote back . . . And when I returned in the winter, he met me at Newark Airport looking like someone who had barely survived Dachau. He looked so bad he scared me.

All of my 'Earth Mother' instincts woke right up. Believe me, I had no intention of loving him—I was there to be his friend in need. I had also decided I was going to be 'off' love that semester. I was going to be serious, chaste, industrious, unapproachable . . . and eat only whole-grain foods.

We spent a lot of time together. He needed someone he could cry in front of; I needed someone who would make me feel a little less self-involved. Things worked out fine.

That was the year he set a school record for scoring and, hate sports as much as I did, I went to as many games as possible. At the beginning I sat in the stands and did my homework, but I couldn't help admiring how smooth and graceful he looked on the court. Soon I stopped doing my homework, became a great fan and knew more about basketball than a serious girl should.

When college was over, Danny was offered two tryouts with professional teams, but true to his Marco Polo nature, he decided to play for a team in Milan instead. I thought it was a nice idea but nuts at the same time—and had no hesitation in telling him that. He shrugged and said he didn't want to play basketball for the rest of his life anyway, so here was a way he could play and see things at

5

the same time without the pressure and worry of big-time American pro sports.

European pro basketball turned out to be rough and often about as subtle as a brick over the head. The finesse and ballet of the game at its best in the United States is lost. American players who come over are often appalled at the steamroller way they go at it in the 'elegant' part of the world.

Danny's letters to me that first year abroad were full of wonderful descriptions of games played in youth centres, military bases, gymnasiums that doubled as town halls. The team gave him a car that blew up, and just enough money to keep his elephant's appetite at bay.

I was working for a magazine in New York as a researcher and feeling lonely most of the time. Live in New York when you're rich or in love, but avoid it when all you have is a job, a smelly apartment on Tenth Street and an empty dance card. That was the year I spent devouring all the books you're only supposed to read at the beach in the summer. I learned how to cook, and thanked God someone had had the compassion to invent television.

During the day I would call places like Alaska and ask distant-voiced scientists about the mating habits of the musk-ox. I was good at my job because I had too much time on my hands and didn't mind putting in extra hours, asking a million extra questions and making perfect copies of my research reports.

I dated a bunch of men with names like Richard and Christopher (multi-syllable names were 'in' again) who, when taken together, didn't add up to one Danny James. His letters from Italy were full of freshness and life. The guys I was seeing were trying their damnedest to be cool and wise and infallible. They took me to grim Bulgarian movies (in the original language) and then explained the story to me afterwards in lousy coffee-houses. Danny liked to talk about the funny mistakes he'd made and how silly he'd looked or felt as a result. He would write a whole letter about a meal of bad pasta that would make me laugh out loud. So many of the sentences had his face. Unfortunately for the Richards and Christophers, I would inevitably receive one of these treasured letters a few hours before a date with one of them and, as a result, I'd be a grump all night.

Yet, just before summer arrived that year, I did something incredibly stupid. Tired of being efficient by day and lonely by night, I went to bed with a beautiful German photographer named Peter

6

(pronounced 'Pay-ter') who made me swoon in my seat the first time he entered the office. Casual affairs had always repelled me, but I had never really experienced lust at first sight. I slept with him on our second date. He took me out for dinner in a very tall building that had a view over all of Manhattan. We ate the most delicious things on the menu and he talked about the ruins of Petra, the game the Afghanis play called *bushkhazi*, an evening he'd spent at a café in Alexandria with Lawrence Durrell.

He never looked me in the eye once in all the times we went to bed in the next months. He preferred to rest his handsome chin on my shoulder every time we 'made love'. He wasn't good and he wasn't bad: he was just 'Pay-ter' who told wonderful stories and expected you to do more than he did once you were in bed. Since there was little else in my life then besides letters from the distant Danny James, I convinced myself I was in love with Peter.

Psychologists say you should never go food shopping when you're hungry, because at that point everything you see looks delicious and you buy strictly on impulse. Popcorn, oysters . . . it doesn't make any sense because your stomach is saying yes to everything, whether it's logical or nutritious or just junk. I met Peter when I was hungry and everything he was looked like a feast.

When I found out I was pregnant, it took me three days to get up the nerve to tell Peter. He told me I was lovely and a wonder, but it wasn't love; he said he had a friend who knew a good abortionist. I said I would do my own shopping around and did. I was too young and sure of my wonderful future to think about losing the child. Somewhere far-off in my mind I knew I wanted to have children later in life, but not now. Not with a man who didn't love me—and not with my mind full of fear and anger and blinking red lights.

What I remember most about the whole experience was the serene sense of comfort and soft calm I felt when I woke up in a hospital bed late one August afternoon, childless again. I never wanted to leave that bed with its crunchy-white sheets and buttery light pouring in through the window.

I went back to my small apartment and opened a magazine. The first thing I saw was a photograph of a family having a picnic in a bright green meadow. I think I looked at that picture for ten minutes. I had left a child in that hospital. I didn't want the child, even with that photograph in my aching lap, but that didn't matter. I felt

7

like there was nothing left—not someone I loved, not a child *of* that love, nothing.

I didn't go mad or anything so dramatic, but I did fall into a depression as deep and dark as the sea at night. I became even more efficient at my job and started reading books on advanced mathematics and architecture when I went home at night. I wanted to keep my mind filled with things that were clean and sharp and logical: pictures of buildings that rose straight off the earth like rockets.

I went to a woman analyst who told me I was beautiful and witty and absolutely right to abort because my body was my own. But her feminist pep-talks only made me sadder and less sure of myself than before. I didn't want to be independent; I wanted to love someone and feel comfortable with my life.

One night I realized that the only person I knew who could come close to understanding my confusion was Danny. So I sat down and wrote him a ten-page, single-spaced letter telling him about my relationship with Peter and the abortion and how it was affecting me. I so vividly remember going to the post office the next day to mail it. After I'd slipped it into the box, I closed my eyes very tightly and said, 'Please, please, please.'

A week later I received a telegram from Milan saying: 'WHY DID YOU WAIT TO TELL ME? THE FIRST THING I'M GOING TO DO IS PUNCH YOU IN THE NOSE. ARRIVING TUESDAY FLIGHT 60/TWA/KENNEDY.'

I spent the entire weekend rushing around shopping, cleaning my apartment (twice), shaking my head in disbelief that Danny was actually arriving in a few days. What was even more unbelievable was that from all accounts, his trip was in response to my confused letter. Did people still rush to another's side to help and comfort? My whole spirit clapped its hands at the thought.

Riding out to the airport on the bus, I kept smoothing the wrinkles in my new dress and said again and again under my breath, 'Flight 60 TWA. Flight 60 TWA.'

The plane was forty-five minutes late in arriving and by the time people started emerging through the gate, I think I'd gone to the bathroom three times. I waited and waited; had gone up and down on my tiptoes a hundred times before I saw this wonderful, familiar giant emerge behind all the other pygmy passengers.

8

He bent down and gave me a big kiss on the lips. His smile was like sitting by a warm fire with the best book you've ever read.

'That's the first time I ever kissed you like that, isn't it? How come I waited so long?'

'And how come you're so tall? I forgot, sort of.'

We walked towards the exit and I had to take two steps to match his every one. I kept looking up at him to make sure he was really there and not just in my best dreams. I envied no one else in the world.

Outside, waiting for a cab to take us back to the city, he towered over everyone with both his height and his pure calm. People screeched and ran by, buses blatted smoke thick as lead, planes carved the air overhead. Danny stood there and smiled at it all.

'You know, it's nice to be back in horrible old New York, Cullen.'

I got up on tiptoes and gave him a big smooch on his sandy cheek. 'Only you would get a kick out of this mess.'

A shabby Checker cab rambled up and the driver came out so fast I thought he'd been catapulted.

'The city? You goin' inna city? Hah?'

'How much?'

'We go the meter! What, you think I'm a crook or somethin'?'

Cab-drivers in New York are either autistic or philosophers; there's rarely an in-between. We'd happened on a philosopher-complainer who kept yakking the whole forty minutes into town. That was nothing new, but Danny yakked right back. The driver's name was Milton Stiller and by the time we were shimmying over the Tri-Borough Bridge, Danny was calling him 'Milt' and asking pertinent questions about his wife, Sylvia.

There are people who will talk to anyone and find something interesting in them. I'm not one of them, but I learned fast that Danny was. People felt comfortable and at home with him, innately sensing he'd neither judge nor betray their confidences, no matter what they were. Our new friend Milton had probably been griping his woes at captive customers for twenty years. But Danny listened and talked and was the kind of human being we all want to kidnap and take home for ever and never share with anyone else. Milt invited us over to dinner just before we got out in front of our apartment house. He said he knew Sylvia would love us.

Danny paid and over-tipped so much my eyes bulged out of my head. He picked up his bags and moved towards the sidewalk.

'Hey, Colon. Come here a minute.'

I'd never been called 'Colon' before. Colin, usually. Even Collar once, but Colon was a new one.

'Yes, Milt?'

'You take care of that big boy, you hear me? Christ, I wish *my* son was like him.'

Fast tears came to my eyes and I had to turn away quickly or else he would have seen me with a very wet face.

'I will. I promise.'

Danny stood at the door with his suitcases and his smile. He was waiting for me: Colon.

The table was set. I brought out the only *pièce de résistance* I knew how to make well—spinach lasagne. As I walked to the table, I suddenly realized something and would have smacked myself on the forehead if I'd had another hand.

'Oh *hell!*'

Danny lowered his glass of beer from his lips, leaving a white foam moustache. 'What's the matter? Did you forget something?'

'Oh Danny, I made *lasagne!* I completely forgot about what you eat in Italy. You must have this three times a day there!'

He shook his head and gestured for me to put it down. Then he bent his head over like a long-necked bird and scrutinized it.

'Cullen it's . . . *green.'* He smiled beatifically.

'Of course it is! It's spinach lasagne.'

'Spinach? Oh.'

'Yes, spinach. I'm a vegetarian. That doesn't mean it's not good.'

'Uh . . . oh.' He was about to take a sip of beer, but put the glass back on the table very gently.

'What's the matter with that? This is the first time I've felt like crying all day.'

'Don't do that. It's just that vegetarians make me nervous.'

'War wouldn't make you nervous, Danny James. Do you enjoy eating dead flesh?'

'Uh . . . oh.' He took his fork and poked at my masterpiece as if he were inspecting a minefield. 'Is it *really* good?'

I squinted flame and acid his way and forked him up a piece as big as a manhole cover. It sat firm and proud . . . and green on his plate.

'You eat that!'

'But it might be hot. Green things stay hot longer, you know.'
'Eat!'

His smile fell but he began to eat and three helpings later he was still going strong. He hadn't said another word, but his face had relaxed and his cheeks stayed full. I know because I watched him like a hawk.

'So how is it, Popeye?'

He patted his tummy. 'I stand corrected; spinach lasagne wins! So what's for dessert, kelp cake?'

'I should feel insulted now, but I'm still too glad to see you. You're a wonderful friend for coming, Danny.'

He bowed his head my way and pushed a spoon a little to the left. 'Are you okay, Cullen?'

'I'm a lot better since I got the telegram saying you were coming. Overall? I'm much better now. I think about the child sometimes, but that's only natural.'

He put his hands in his lap and leaned forward as if he were about to whisper a secret. 'I know it's easy for me to say it, but I don't think you should worry about that if you can help it, Cul. You aborted because you had to. You didn't love the man, I'm assuming. What better reason could you have had than that?'

'Oh, Danny, I know. I've run all that through my mind, but it *was* a person in there. There's no way I can get around that.' Tears came to my eyes. It seemed I wasn't over anything yet.

Danny shook his head and looked at me very sternly. Then one of his hands came up from his lap and he placed it on the table in a tight fist. 'You're wrong, Cullen. The seed *isn't* the flower. I'm not trying to be facile either. What kind of life would that child have had? Huh? Even if you *had* wanted it, there would have been so many times you'd have resented the poor thing and your decision to have it. Look at our parents and how many times they wanted to brain *us* when we were growing up. All my life I've heard people say it's a nip-and-tuck battle for parents to love their kids all the way through. As good a person as I think you are, I do think you would have scarred the kid somehow. It may not be a very nice thing for me to say, but we really *don't* need any more walking wounded on this earth, you know?'

'I'm not saying you're in any way wrong, Danny, but life just isn't that simple. If it was as easy and clear cut as you say . . . If it was as logical as that, I wouldn't continue to feel as bad as I do. I know

11

what you're saying, and you're absolutely right in a way. *But* logic and rationality only go so far. Then you know what happens? Ha! Then your old heart adds its two cents and everything reasonable goes right-out-the-window.'

I took out a cigarette and lit up. We were quiet, comfortably quiet for a while. Even with talk of the baby, I felt more at ease than I had in ages.

Danny sighed and frowned. 'You're right, Cullen. A hundred per cent right. Remember how I was after Evelyn died? Every time I tried to tell myself to just calm down and get back to living my life, my emotions said, "Fuck you, Buddy, we hurt!"'

It was not a funny thought, but the way he said it made me grin. He grinned back and I reached across the table and took his hand.

'You know something funny? You almost always blow smoke out of the side of your mouth, Cul. I remember that from before. Are you aware of it?'

'Huh?'

'You shoot the smoke out the side; like you're making a little comment or something. Never in front.'

'Now I'm going to be self-conscious.'

'Cullen, you're the prettiest woman I know. You have every right to be self-conscious.'

He said that without any hesitation, but wouldn't look at me when he did. How many good men are there in the world who are both shy and complimentary at the same time? The men I'd gone out with recently were full of both compliments and eye contact, but I often got the feeling neither meant a damn.

He took a coin out of his pocket and did a lovely little trick with it —flash, whoosh, gone!—just for me.

'That's neat, Dan. Do it again!'

'Nope! Never ask a magician to do his tricks twice in a row. You'll figure them out and they'll lose all their magic that way.'

I went into the kitchen to get the dessert—a giant, horrendously gooey chocolate cake that looked great and broke all the rules.

Danny's whole face lit up as soon as he saw it. That night marked the beginning of our many-year contest to see who had the greater madness for sweets.

When I put it down on the table, he reached over and pulled the whole thing in front of him. 'Oh Cullen, that was really nice of you to get this for me. And what are you having for dessert?'

12

Over coffee and cake we talked about everything. His words were so like his letters; taking their time to get wherever, funny, self-deprecating. It was plain he saw himself as a hell of a lucky guy who had been plopped down in a fascinating, illogical world for no reason other than to have a good look around, hands in pockets and a little surprised whistle on his lips.

Years before, I had taken his 'way' for naïvety when I first knew him, but it wasn't that. It was a healthy, magnificently unpolluted sense of wonder. Life was wonderful—or at least full of wonders—for Danny James. He would look at a junkyard and be thrilled by the weird mix of colours in there. When he prodded me into looking, I would see a junkyard. Not a good or a bad one, simply a junkyard! Yet his wonder was not annoying or particularly contagious either. Most of the time you didn't even know it was there until you looked up at him and saw those quiet brown eyes staring at whatever it was, a slight, pleased smile on his face.

I grew to hope for that smile; it was really the only way I could tell what was going on in his mind. As I've said before, it was very hard to tell when he was mad about something, and only slightly less difficult to tell when he was happy. His wasn't a stone face, exactly, but rather a handsome one with a set, bemused expression that rarely changed, and kept secrets—both his and your own—like no one else I had ever known.

'Well, Dan, now you're going to have to spill the beans: have you been gallivanting around Italy with contessas?'

'No, no contessas. Not many of them go to basketball games. There *is* this one woman . . .' His voice trailed off and he looked away. Embarrassed?

'Yes, all right; there's this one woman. *And?*' Unconsciously I took out another cigarette. I was smoking up to two packs a day and climbing; before the abortion it had been less than one.

He looked at me, smiled, shrugged. 'It's very hard for me, Cullen. Believe it or not, since Evelyn died I have been very low-keyed with women. I go to bed with some and some go to bed with me—if you get the difference—but a lot less than some people think. Until recently I've had no desire to jump into any . . . pool and get wet. There've been other interesting things to pay attention to, like living in Europe for one. I think it's going to be a very slow process, finding someone else to be with for the rest of my life.'

I had the cigarette in my mouth and was squinting against the

13

smoke that curled up the side of my cheek. 'But now you sound like you think you found someone.'

'I don't know. I've spent a lot of time thinking about it, believe me. To tell you the truth, most of the time women make me nervous. Really! I often feel like I'm either saying the wrong thing or acting the wrong way—even when I know they like me. Isn't that silly? I feel like a kid going to dance class for the first time; which hand do I put where on the girl's body?'

We smiled at each other and the room hummed with comfort and companionship.

'But you were married once, Danny. You should know all the ropes.'

'Maybe some of them, but really I was only married long enough to know I liked it, Cul. Then it went away.'

'Danny, you're smart and you've got a good heart, so answer me this, will you? Why do all the jerks do so well in life? And why do so many nice people get stomped on? If anyone didn't deserve to lose their wife, it's you.'

'It's not that simple, Cullen. Sometimes it works out fine.' His voice was soft and sad.

'Oh yeah? Well, I don't think it works out fine too often. Do you want more cake? Say yes, please.'

'Of course.'

The new woman's name was Drew Conrad. Whoever heard of a girl named Drew? But she was a model and that explained a lot about her, as far as I was concerned. Every guy I knew in those days was going out with a model. My definition of a model? Airheads with nice teeth.

'What's she doing in Italy, besides posing?'

'Are you telling me that you don't like models? Why don't you do it, Cullen? You sure could make more money than you do at that magazine. God knows, you've certainly got the looks for it!'

'Yeah, I'm pretty, but when people look it makes me extremely nervous. What's more, I wouldn't want to spend my life posing on a car-hood in a pair of purple underpants. Hey, guys, look what you can have if you buy that Fiat! It's tacky, Danny. I'm sure not the world's best person, but I work hard to avoid being tacky if I can. Modelling *reeks* of tack. Look, I'm sorry if I'm squashing your Drew Conrad. Are you going to tell me what she's like?'

'She's tall and dark. We met at a party in Milan.'

14

'And?'

'And . . . well, um, the sex is nice.'

'And?' For the first time, the question of what Danny James would be like in bed crossed my mind. I looked hard at him and imagined he guessed what I was thinking because he quickly averted his eyes and scrooched around in his chair like he had ants in his pants.

But I liked sex. I also liked my aloe plant and the International House of Pancakes. My experiences with sex reminded me of a great new movie that everyone talks about and loves. You go along hoping, *hoping* it will be everything they said it was. But then it's over and you walk out of the theatre, blinking hard at the sudden light— tired, and sort of disappointed and confused by all the hoopla the thing has received.

Most of my bedroom stories could have been divided into two simple categories: 'Bunny Rabbit Sex' and 'Blackmail Sex'. I'd had scads of Bunny Rabbit Sex—crazily eager, jackhammer stuff so repetitious and unoriginal that your nose started twitching in frustration after a while.

Or there was the ever-popular Blackmail Sex: do it with me right now or else I'll be depressed for the rest of my life . . . or at least the rest of tonight. 'Pay-ter' was a great one for that and I fell for it each time.

Now, sizing up Danny in a sexy light, I couldn't imagine him being guilty of either approach, but like him as much as I did, I still had my doubts.

'Cullen, did I say something wrong?'

'No, nothing, Danny. I was just thinking about sex.'

His eyes smiled and he winked the nicest wink that ever was. 'Cullen, I wouldn't know what to do if you and I went to bed. You know why? I'd be too busy staring at you to think of anything else.'

It was said with such great humour and warmth that the only thing I wanted to do was get up and give him a hug, which I did. He hugged back and the next thing I knew, I was crying all over his gigantic shoulder.

'I don't want to cry, but I can't really help it.'

He squeezed me tighter and stroked the back of my head again and again. It was a wonderful feeling. He also had that man's bouquet of smells—heat, cologne, sweat, summer earth. It made you

15

hot, comfortable; assured you that for a moment or two you would be safe from the snapping alligator jaws of life.

Don't get me wrong—good smells or not, putting your arms around most men was either like embracing a chimp or a tombstone. Men either 'let' you hug them or quickly tried to turn that nicest of things into an orgy.

Not Danny James. His hands ran down my back in innocent rills that I wished would go on for ever. Hands are wonderful; they can disappear coins, or they can iron out wrinkles in blue, rumpled souls.

'Are you crying because you're so sad to see me, Cul?'

I smiled and sniffed into his chest. His words, his hands on my back, his *presence* there was like someone had opened a trap-door in the top of my head and poured warm milk in, filling my body, soaking all of my cells, soothing them all with its life, vitamins, whiteness.

I told him this and he chuckled. 'I've never been called a glass of milk before.'

Jet-lag caught up with him an hour later and he started yawning. I steered him into the bathroom and told him that by the time he was finished in there, I'd have the couch made up and he could flop right down and go to sleep. He shuffled out a few minutes later wearing a pair of cute flannel pyjamas as big as an Indian tepee.

'The couch is all made up. I'll get out of here and let you go to sleep.'

'Cullen, I'm going to sleep with you. Don't say no, and don't think I'm going to try anything. I came a hell of a long way to see you, so we're not going to play any games with each other. We'll sleep and be good, but we'll be sleeping together. Okay?'

'Okay.' I couldn't look at him and my heart was beating very fast.

'That "okay" didn't sound so good.'

'OKAY!'

'Good. I'm completely exhausted. I'll see you later. Thank you for dinner, even if it was green.' He turned and started out.

'Danny? I'm so glad you're here.'

'Me too.' He half-turned and gave a little tired wave.

I watched him scuff off into the bedroom and lie down, Gulliver-style, on my surprised bed. Then I went into the kitchen and did the dishes with worried hands.

Naturally, nothing happened when I did get into bed. Danny was

16

sound asleep. Rolling over on my side, I smiled into the darkness and listened for a long time to the hiss of his breathing.

I awoke when I felt a hand on my face and opened my eyes to see Danny looking at me from ten inches away. His face was puffed and crinkled into a sleepy smile.

'I think I'm jet-lagged. It's nine in the morning where I live so I'm wide awake!'

Without a thought, I slid over and put my arms around his big sleep-warmed body. We lay there for a little while and then fell asleep again.

The next time I awoke I smelled good things in the air, but was disappointed to discover he wasn't there to smell them with me.

I like men's shoulders. Always have. The first thing I saw of Danny that morning was his shoulders moving and jumping around as he worked at the stove cooking breakfast. I leaned against the door and watched while he moved here and there amidst cooking sounds and flying hands. He seemed to know exactly what to do. And he had great shoulders. High and broad, they spanned the top of a thin, well-kept body. I had spent the night with that body and the thought made me smile; I had never slept with anyone without fooling around before. I felt like a newly-minted coin. What had happened last night reminded me of a story out of the Middle Ages: one of those great ones, where the virtuous knight sleeps with his lady-fair in the same bed, only he's placed his trusty sword between them on the sheets to keep them both virtuous.

The only part of the story that didn't fit so well was that Ms Drew Conrad was Danny's lady-fair at the moment, while I was just his pal in need.

Had I fallen a little in love with him only because part of me was nasty-competitive, or because everything he'd done since he'd arrived the day before had been supremely adorable?

Without knowing I was there, he turned on the radio to a disco station. Spatula in hand, he started dancing around. He was pretty good.

'Do you have any pictures of you when you were a little girl?'

I was startled that he'd known all along that I was there. He turned around and, flipping the spatula, caught it with two fingers.

'You're a real bag of tricks, aren't you? Pictures of me when I was little? Yes, I have a big bunch of them somewhere in a drawer.'

'Terrific! Let's eat first and then you can get them out for me.'

'How come you want to see them?' I sat down at the table. He'd already taken my usual spot, but I liked to see him sitting there.

'I want to see if you were as pretty then as you are now.'

He said this while putting a plate of scrambled eggs, toast and sliced tomato in front of me. There was even a thin sprig of bright green parsley laid over the eggs. It added an unnecessary, albeit lovely touch of colour and care to the whole thing that made it a hundred times better. Danny *cared;* for the food he cooked, for me . . . for everything.

'I'm not used to being told I'm good-looking.' Very unprettily, I shovelled a large load of food into my mouth.

'Men don't tell you because they don't want to admit your advantage over them. The better-looking a woman is, the more insecure a man gets.'

'Why's that? How ridiculous! Would you pass the salt?'

'Because it's hard to walk down the street with someone who makes other people walk into walls when they look. Plus, no one looks at *you* when you're with that pretty person. It's very humbling.'

'Is Drew Conrad pretty?' I stopped chewing and realized my fork was hanging in mid-air.

He hesitated a moment, then nodded bashfully, but he wouldn't look at me.

'What advertisements has she done? Anything over here I would have seen?'

'I don't know—all of the big ones, I think. They brought her over from New York, so I guess she's known over here too.'

'Do you bump into walls when you see *her?'*

'Every so often.'

I pushed my plate away a little too hard and it skidded across the table like a hockey puck. 'Okay! All right, I admit it—I'm jealous. No, I *hate* her, Dan! I look at you and I'm thinking there are neat men in the world. Look, there's one right here in front of me. So where the hell are they? All I ever meet are squeenys and mudballs.'

'What's a squeeny?'

'Hey, just walk into any Singles' Bar and take your pick. Computer dating. The New York Review of Books Classified Section: "Docile Virgo seeking intrepid Lion to run through the dunes with." After some time in that world, "Pay-ter" seemed like Clark Gable.'

A big silence followed. I was beginning to worry that once again I'd somehow put my foot in my big mouth, when Danny finally spoke.

'Cullen, there's no Drew Conrad!'

'*What?*'

'Just what I said. She's what you might call a figment of my perverse imagination.'

'Danny, what *are* you talking about?'

'Nothing. It's just that there's no Drew Conrad. I made her up. *Basta.* That's all!'

My spirit hoisted five flags. 'But why? Whatever for?'

'Whatever for, Cullen? Because the truth of the matter is, I'm scared to death of you!'

'Of *me?* James, are you cracked? Look at me, damn it!'

He sighed and looked at me with the saddest expression in town. 'It's very simple, don't you see? If I had a woman like Drew to tell you about, then we would be on safe ground. You wouldn't have to worry about someone else being forward with you. And if I pretended convincingly enough that she *did* exist, then I was hoping you wouldn't see how gone I am for you. See, Cullen, I had it all figured out: I would just rhapsodize about you, but call you Drew Conrad, and I'd be all set.'

His face had the calmness of truth in it. He looked me in the eye while he spoke and after a while *I* was the one who began to feel uncomfortable.

'When you wrote me about your abortion, I realized I had been in love with you for a long time. Maybe even when we were in college, right at the end of senior year! Anyway, when I got your letter over there and I started imagining you alone in that hospital bed having to go through such an ordeal . . .'

I was a few feet away from him but I could plainly see there were tears in his eyes. Tears for me! Who had ever cried for me? What man had ever cared so much?

My heart turned in my chest, but the tears and obvious depth of his emotion scared me and made me want to be alone so I could catch my breath and think all this over for a minute, an hour, a few days.

'I'm sorry, Cullen. I *really* don't want to create any more problems for you. I promised myself I wouldn't tell you any of this.' He got up tiredly from the table and walked into the bedroom, closing the door behind him.

Loving someone is easy. It's your car and all you have to do is start the engine, give her a little gas and point the thing wherever you want to go. But being loved is like being taken for a ride in someone else's car. Even if you think they'll be a good driver, you always have the innate fear they might do something wrong: in an instant you'll both be flying through the windshield towards imminent disaster. Being loved can be the most frightening thing of all. Because love means goodbye to control; and what happens if halfway or three-quarters of the way through the trip you decide you want to go back, or in a different direction, and you're only the co-driver?

DUMB! You wanted to be loved, Cullen? Loved by a special, wonderful man? Okay, here you are—right in your hand. What happens? What's your reaction? You get scared. Dumb!

I rubbed my face with both hands and snorted at my stupidity.

'Danny?'

No answer.

'Danny!'

The door opened slowly and reluctantly. He stood there stooped in his dandy green pyjamas, vulnerable and from the look on his face, expecting the worst.

'Please don't say anything sweet, Cullen. Don't be sweet or pitying; I couldn't take that.'

'Come in here and finish your breakfast.'

His . . . I don't know what you would call it . . . declaration? Anyway, it did funny things to us. Made us shy of each other, but very intimate at the same time. When we were walking down the street a few hours later, he took my hand, which sent a bolt of flaming orange lightning across my brain. What courage it must have taken for him to do that! To reach right over and take my hand, after what he had said with no response from me one way or the other . . . I'd wanted to grab hold of his hand too, but hadn't had the guts to do it in that still, tense interval in our relationship between nothing and everything.

We did too many things that day. Walked everywhere, saw this, saw that, ate everything. Both of us knew the whole time that if we kept good and busy, we could temporarily skirt the issue at hand. I think that's what we both wanted.

New York is good for that. It has everything to show you and never enough time in any day to do it all. We took a subway to the Brooklyn Bridge and walked along the Promenade, looking at the harbour. We were holding hands by then and both of us held on tight, but made as little eye contact as possible. We were acting like fourteen-year-old jerks, and since both of us were suddenly so shy with each other, it reminded me of how people must have courted back in *Friendly Persuasion* times.

For the first time, I asked Danny about his family. His father was dead, but his mother and sister lived in North Carolina. This was surprising, because he spoke with no southern accent at all. When I mentioned this, he said he had lived in New Jersey until he was fifteen. Then his father—who was a furniture designer—was offered a job in North Carolina at one of those big furniture firms down there. The family moved to a small town named Hickory which was the home of the factory. Nine months later, Mr James had a cerebral haemorrhage at work and that was that.

Mrs James got a job teaching at a local private school and her income—along with her husband's life insurance money—enabled the family to settle into a comfortable, sad way of life. Danny went to college on a basketball scholarship.

The boats in New York harbour shuffled and steamed and chuffed from side to side in the open water and in their dark berths. Boats that had been on the high seas for months, loaded down with enough bananas or Spanish shoes or Japanese watercolour sets to keep the city going for ever. I looked on those boats and realized for the zillionth time that I had never been anywhere in the world outside of Chicago, New Brunswick, New Jersey and New York City. The only Greece I knew was *souvlaki* and posters of the Parthenon in a tired Greek restaurant I liked on 46th Street. I had never owned a passport, never needed a visa. The only Europe I had ever known was through sleeping with a European. The only adventure I had ever had was an abortion.

'Danny, what's it like living over there?'

'Like? Well, you always find odd coins in your pockets. You'll be looking for a hundred lira and you'll find five francs in there instead. You think you're giving a guy five schillings for a newspaper and it turns out to be five drachma.'

21

'Drachma. Have you been to Greece too? God, I hate you. What's it like?'

'Athens is loud and messy. But the islands are exactly what you'd hoped for.'

'And London?'

'Dirty.'

'Vienna?'

'Very clean and very grey. Are we playing "Twenty Questions"?'

We were sitting on a bench watching the day's traffic float by: those boats in the harbour, parents with baby strollers, old men moving slowly and complaining to the air.

'No, but Danny, what's it *like?* Is it all that different? Is the world really different over there?'

'Why? What's the matter, Cullen?'

'Oh, I don't know. I want things to change, Danny. You know? I want to look out of my window in the morning and see . . . and see orange street-cars!'

'Those are in Milan.' He smiled and took my hand in both of his.

'All right, see, they do exist! I want orange street-cars, or book-sellers along the river selling books in Italian or Hungarian or some other language I can't understand. I want to sit in a café with marble tables and eat a real croissant. Oh Danny, I know I'm being a big brat, but I'd do anything to see those things. I really would!'

'Then why don't you go to Europe?'

'Because I'm a chicken, that's why! I don't want to be disappointed. And I never had anyone I wanted to go with, but basically because I'm a chicken.'

He licked his lips and then pressed them tightly together. Whatever he was about to say was going to be hard for him.

'Come and stay with me in Italy, Cullen. We'll do all the things you want, together. You keep saying you don't like your job or living in New York. So come to Milan for as long as you want and I'll treat you to as many rides as you want on orange street-cars.'

'Things sure happen fast sometimes, don't they?'

'Uh-huh. But you know, I'm totally serious about this. I want you to come, if *you* want!'

I took hold of him and hugged him, right there on that park bench. Hugged him with all of the strength I had. Not because it was the end of the movie and we were about to live happily ever after. And not because it was his way of proposing to me and both

22

of us knew it. Mostly it was because he had reaffirmed to me that there *were* such things as orange street-cars in the world and some time soon, no matter what finally happened between us, we would be seeing those things together.

We didn't make love until the night before he left. We kissed a lot and touched and *slept* together, but none of the big stuff until we only had a few hours left. That fact—notwithstanding the happiness and excitement (and speed!) of our new bond—scared us into the final, ultimate act of affirmation.

There's no reason to go into any detail about that night, but there were a few things he did that knocked me for a loop.

The first was that he didn't actually enter me for ages. For the longest time he seemed content just to touch and kiss and, true to his word, look at me. I wasn't used to the slowness of everything. Peter and my other horizontal acquaintances were always hurrying. Hurrying to get undressed, hurrying to get hot, hurrying to begin the 'Main Event'. But beside the fact that hurrying often hurt me physically because I wasn't ready for them, I kept thinking that there ought to be some subtlety in it; subtlety and gentleness, and many minutes invested in an act that *could* mean a very great deal if you really worked at it, rather than just bounced on it. Too often I had spent my time staring at designs on different ceilings while a hot little human locomotive pounded his way inside me towards . . . who knows where?

Danny was not the best lover I had ever had, but he was by far the most generous. He touched and stroked me until I was slick with sweat and hope. And when he finally did enter me, I had to urge him to do it. As he did, he asked me two or three times if he was hurting me. The expression on his face said he was very concerned about that. I touched his cheek and said it felt great.

He put his head next to mine and whispered in my ear, ' "It" doesn't feel great. *You* feel great!'

When he came, he arched his back like a diver going off a high board. But he was looking right at me and I don't think he took his eyes off me the whole time. As he moved very hard up and through me he said, he hissed with a smile on his face a mile wide, 'It's a *song*, Cullen!'

*

The next morning he was leaning up on one elbow and smiling at me when I opened my eyes. I smiled back and reached out my arms for him. He came over and I took hold of him and rocked him back and forth. He was twice as big as me, but right then he felt weightless; as if I could hold all of him in one hand.

'How do you feel, Cul?'

'Terrific. I'm only sad that you're going.'

'And last night?'

'Sleeping together? It was lovely.'

'You're sure?'

'Absolutely.'

We lazed around for a while and then he got up. 'Stay where you are. I have a surprise.'

A half hour later he came in with a tray full of fresh croissants, fruit, hard-boiled eggs, and coffee in two ceramic mugs I had never seen before. One was red, the other green. Best of all, there was an old book of Italian fairy tales—in Italian.

'See, you don't even have to go to Europe to get the croissants and books in Italian! The mugs are a going-away present. You get the green and I get the red. If you let anyone else drink from my mug, I'll poke you in the nose!' His voice was playful, but the expression on his face was the first and last hint he ever gave that said he fully expected me to remain faithful to him. Not faithful so much in body, although that was part of it, but faithful more to the idea of what had been growing between us since he had arrived.

'I know what you're saying, Danny, but please don't make little veiled threats like that. They're not necessary and you make me feel sleazy. I'm not *that* bad.'

He put the tray beside me on the bed and sat himself down on the floor. We ate in an uncomfortable silence that made me quickly lose my appetite.

He shouldn't have threatened and I shouldn't have snapped. The sound of a spoon stirring coffee never rang so loudly as it did in those few long minutes of grim silence. Happiness, contentment, peace: all three of those things balance perched on the point of the thinnest pin. The slightest movement of the earth knocks them off —and boy, how they crash when they hit!

'Cullen, I want to tell you a story because the last thing I want is for you to misunderstand what I'm getting at.

24

'When I was a little boy, my father took me for a ride in the country one day, just the two of us. We drove alongside a lake for a few miles and then suddenly, out of nowhere, a bunch of ducks flew low out of the trees by the side of the road. My father hit the whole bunch, square on . . . all of them.'

Both of us had our hands wrapped around the coffee mugs. I looked down at Danny to see what this story had to do with the argument of a minute ago. But he was looking off into space and the steam from his coffee was being blown here and there by the strength of his breath.

'Dad pulled the car over and we got out to see what had happened. It was a mess. Real carnage . . . blood and feathers were splattered across the whole front of the car. Even as a little boy I knew the sight upset him. He picked up the bodies—there were four of them—and threw them as far off the road and into the woods as he could. We were out in the middle of nowhere, so there was no way we could clean the car, which by then looked as if it had come through some kind of massacre. Our ride in the country was ruined, so Dad turned the car around and drove us straight home.

'But here's the real macabre part. As we drove up our driveway, my mother was coming out of the house with a load of washing under her arm to hang up on the line. She took one look at the front of the car and started screaming. And I mean *screaming,* Cul—not little "ohs" and "ahs" or something like that. These were screams and shouts, real hysteria! Dad and I were so shocked by it that we forgot for a moment what she was so obviously screaming about— the blood and guts that were still splattered across the front of the car! We simply thought she had flipped her lid.

'Dad slammed on the brakes and both of us jumped out. Mom started shouting, "Who did you kill? Oh God, who did you kill?" Then she fell down on her knees and started moaning. Wow, I'll never forget that scene as long as I live! Sooner or later it dawned on us what she was raving about and we got her cooled down. But for a while it was frightening as hell. She was completely out of control.'

He sipped his coffee and silently I waited for him to go on. The picture of his mother down on her knees and the bloody, dripping car grille made me uneasy and trembly.

'The reason why I'm telling you this terrible story, Cullen, is because my father was a horrendous driver. Seeing all that blood on the car wasn't the only reason my mother had just gone crazy. For years she had been on at Dad in a nice way to be careful, because he was so bad behind the wheel. He never looked at the road, always drove too fast, never used his indicators . . . Even as a kid I knew I was taking my life in my hands when I went out riding with him, although he loved to have us all in the car with him whenever he went somewhere.

'What happened this time was that my mother took one look at the front of the car and all of her years of fearing the worst came together in that one minute. He'd done it: she was sure he'd done what she'd been expecting him to do for years. She was sure he had killed someone. The blood told her everything she needed to know. Do you understand?'

I nodded slowly, still not seeing how all this connected to us.

'Cullen, everything you've been telling me these past few days adds up to your being confused and unsure of who you are in the world. The relationships you've had in the past—especially with that stupid Peter—have only made you *more* unsure. Then the abortion thing topped it all off. Whatever self-esteem or conviction you had left went flying out of the window. You want everything to change now, like you said the other day, because you don't like where you are, either physically or . . . well, spiritually. Am I right?'

'I don't like hearing you say any of this, but you're right.'

'Don't feel that way. I'm not trying to hurt you. If you come to Europe, things *will* change. I promise you that. You'll have your street-cars and you'll have someone who'll take care of you. Me! But in the meantime, I don't want to be like my mother with my father, constantly worrying about you.'

'Worry? Why would you worry about me? What are you saying, Danny?'

'I'm saying that you have got to start knowing that you're good and smart and capable. You can't keep thinking you're a beautiful flunkey who only deserves another flunkey like Peter. I'm not worried about your remaining true to *me*, Cullen; I'm worried about your remaining true to yourself. For God's sake, you're a wonderful woman. I don't know anybody else like you and that's why I love you. But I also know I think more of you than you do of yourself, and that's bad. It's dangerous.

'I don't think I need to say any more, do you?'

26

In April I flew to Athens and on the plane I met a Greek named Lillis, who invited me to visit him on the island of Skiathos. He described how the poppies were just coming into bloom now, and how he would love to take me to Koukounaries beach in his boat to swim in the Aegean. 'Koukounaries' means pine cones in Greek and the Aegean *was* Greece, and half an hour into the flight I realized I was flying to *Greece!* Greece, as in Plato and Sparta and Henry Miller's favourite country. Danny James would be there to meet me and after a two-week tour, we would fly to Milan and take life from there. I was so proud and excited to be doing this and I didn't even mind too much when Lillis got fresh during the movie a few hours later. I told him it was very nice of him, but I was being met in Athens by my seven-foot-tall husband, and that calmed Lillis right down.

I looked out of the window several hundred times, although it was dark out there and you couldn't see a thing. We were flying over the Atlantic Ocean to Europe. I had quit my job, emptied out my savings account, had several yelling matches over the telephone with my mother, and essentially taken my life in my hands. There was courage in those acts, courage and gumption, and I felt reckless and brave and magnificent all at the same time.

When we landed early the next morning, I saw the sea, old propeller planes painted in camouflage and white buildings everywhere. Danny was standing at the gate.

PART TWO

1

Because Greece was the first 'Europe' I had ever known, I loved it like you love your first child: you demand everything of it and what you receive swells your heart like a balloon.

When we returned to Italy after those first two weeks, I had the secret fear that nothing could be as good as those first days overseas. Afternoon light couldn't possibly fall on broken walls the same way as it did in Greece. Where else on earth would someone think of using giant rubber bands to hold the tablecloth down at an outdoor restaurant? On beaches of black sand, men walked alongside ancient mules that carried melons for sale. The men cut the melons in half with one swat of a big knife and the red fruit tasted so sweet and cool in the hot afternoon sun.

And I was right—those things belonged in Greece's house and I gradually learned not to look for them elsewhere. But that was the most wondrous surprise of this new world: you didn't have to look for them, because 'elsewhere' you looked out of the window of your *auberge* in Brittany and saw sheep grazing in salt marshes by the grey ocean. Elsewhere you saw fresh blood on men's faces in Dublin and it made you realize that what you'd once read about the scrappy Irish was true. Elsewhere you felt the cogwheel train carry you up the craggy side of the *Schneeberg* in Austria; half-way there, the train stopped at a tiny station so they could pour water into the boiler of the turn-of-the-century steam locomotive.

Milan was a bunch of bustle and beautiful hidden courtyards. I got a job at Berlitz teaching young Italian go-getters how to speak American. The hours were odd and the majority of my students were snazzy young guys who couldn't decide whether to pay attention to the lesson or try making a little pass at the teacher. We got used to each other and I began learning not to be nervous when life wasn't going exactly as planned.

But getting used to European life was hard. Getting used to European life *and* living with someone for the first time was often a landslide of frustration, responsibility—and days when all I wanted was to quietly go off and ram my head against a wall.

A sample? Danny was a slob, while I was Miss Neat. The first time he shed his clothes as he walked across the room to bed, leaving them in colourful little piles where they fell, I gawked but said nothing. The next time he did it I picked up the things in the morning and put them in his closet. The third time, I screamed. He smiled like he didn't know what I was talking about; said I sounded like Oscar in *The Odd Couple*.

Another thing that drove me crazy about him was that he had no facility for language, but that didn't stop him for a second. He would walk into the corner store and ask in his nice American English for two yams, tabasco sauce, a bit of fresh basil and two cokes. Then he would come home with the two cokes and shrug sweetly: 'I guess they were out of yams, Cul.' I'd be in the middle of making fresh pesto sauce, and more than once found myself throwing the stirring spoon at his retreating head. 'Get back in here and stir this stuff!' I'd grab my Italian dictionary and head for the door, knowing it was partly my fault for sending him in the first place.

When I got mad at Danny, I yelled. When he got mad at me, he either said four concise words or else wrote a note and taped it to the bathroom mirror or my dressing-table.

But the chemistry was right and I learned you can survive without basil so long as you like the person sitting across the table from you at dinner.

He became less of a slob and studied his vocabulary. I grew less hysterical and learned to stop worrying about everything twice.

Other problems? Two o'clock in the afternoon in Italy is fourteen hundred hours. *Quattordici.* Figure that word out when you're in a hurry. Everything was measured in metres and *ettos.* Old friends—words like butter and hot water—had had radical plastic surgery and were suddenly unrecognizable strangers named *burro* and *aqua calda.* Doesn't *calda* sound like *cold?* It did to me. I made that mistake for two weeks running.

You get the gist. I ran around like a squeaky mouse in a cartoon, trying to learn this new language and culture in five minutes, and getting things straight with the man I was falling more and more in love with by the moment.

In the meantime, Dan was tearing up the turf for his basketball team. As with so much else in Italy, the Italian basketball games were raucous, funny and loud as hell. I went to as many as I could. Fans jumped up and down in the stands, slapping their heads in mock dismay and yelling things like *'Mascalzone senze Calzone!'* ('Filth without pants!') at the referee. They brought picnic baskets full of food to the games and shared their things with whoever sat near them. I think I gained four pounds that season, because I always sat in the same section at home games and got to know my neighbours, who always had some new sausage or sweet to eat along with the action. I think they secretly felt that if they fed me, it would give Danny more energy.

Danny said he did so much better that year because of me, and I loved that, but I think he scored so many points and played so wonderfully because he was young and good and living his first adult days in Europe with someone he loved. There isn't much more you can ask for in life, and we often said—in our different ways—how very lucky we were to be there together.

In between games and language classes, we travelled whenever we could: to Florence, Siena, Assisi and Rome. We spent Christmas in a villa on Lake Maggiore with a wonderfully Catholic team member of Danny's who took us (along with his huge family) to mass every morning and told us we had to have at least eleven children.

One night during our stay there, I suddenly started crying like a fool. Very calmly, Danny put down his book and asked what was up.

'I don't know. It's so stupid. I'm just feeling very sad.'

'Anything I can do for you?'

'No, you go to sleep. I'll be all right.'

'Cul, was it something I did?'

'No, of course not! I'm just being a baby. I just want everything to stop right now and never *never* move again: like a picture you carry in your wallet. You know those? The kind people carry in their wallet to show you? Whoever it is, is always smiling and so happy. But you *know* they were always sad after that. Maybe five minutes or a day after the picture was taken, someone they loved died, or they lost their job . . . and everything got screwed up. I just want

33

to freeze everything right now, so nothing will ever change or go wrong with us.'

After basketball season was over, we spent a month driving through Europe in Danny's schizophrenic car. In between breakdowns and new mufflers, we went everywhere. We returned to Milan broke with thirty rolls of undeveloped film and memories galore.

We were married that autumn and promised our parents to fly home the next summer to visit.

The second year started out as gloriously as the first. There was nothing reluctant about life with Danny. He woke up most mornings smiling and ready to go, no matter what day it was. He taught me by his constant example how to charge forward and hope for the best. After much late-night discussion and some tearful scenes, I stopped taking the pill in January. A month later I found out I was pregnant. When I told Danny, he put his hands to his face and said through his fingers that it was the happiest news he had ever had. Inevitably, the pregnancy made me think about my abortion. I wondered if in some cosmic scheme of things, there was any way that I might be giving birth to the child I had purposely lost. The idea was loony and I wasn't about to tell it to Danny, but why wasn't it possible? Who said things like that couldn't happen in life?

I went around feeling great, and eating half of Italy. I felt no hesitation in gorging myself at any time of the day or night, particularly on goodies. Danny once caught me with a candy-bar in each hand. I gained eighteen pounds in four months.

Unlike many pregnant women, I felt fine and full of energy. I even took on more students at Berlitz and the flirting of the year before quickly disappeared when the snazzies saw I was *incinta*.

2

The first of what Danny called my 'Yasmuda dreams' came on a night in early spring in Milan, when we were able to leave the windows open in our bedroom for the first time.

It began with me looking out of the window of an aircraft as it circled some unknown airport. I turned and looked at a child sitting next to me, who I knew immediately was my son. His name was Pepsi. He looked like a little Irishman: curly brown hair, blue eyes full of curiosity and the devil. Instantly, I put my arm around him and pulled him over so that he could look out of the window too. I started talking as the plane began its slow descent.

'I remember when the sea was full of fish with mysterious names: Mudrake, Cornsweat, Yasmuda, and there wasn't much to do in a day. Clouds moved like bows over the sky. Their music was silver and sad. Your father drove a fast little sports car that sounded like a happy bee and he drove me wherever I pleased.'

That was it. That was all that happened, or all I could remember of the dream when I woke the next morning. Danny was already up and after I excitedly told him everything, his only comment was, 'Yasmuda?'

I was proud of my unconscious accomplishment and told him he was just jealous. I got out of bed and wrote down every bit of the dream, which wasn't hard because the words and scene were still so vivid in my mind. I didn't know what any of it meant, but I didn't care. Creating Yasmuda the Fish and a son named Pepsi made me feel strange and very original.

Sometimes dreams bite like fleas and leave little itchy bumps all over your skin. But you know they're not real; you know your brain is only cleaning out its closet . . . But that does no good. The vision, like the flea-bite, raises a bump that is almost impossible to ignore. I wanted to know where the plane was landing; I wanted to know more about Pepsi . . . Pepsi James?

Danny said it was probably my body chemistry moving around, but I didn't buy that. I was convinced something more interesting than that was going on and I wanted to know what.

A few nights later some of the questions were answered. I had two glasses of wine with dinner, which normally made me feel only pleasantly warm. This time they laid a lead blanket over my head and sent me spinning into bed.

'Will there be snow, Mommy?'

'Yes, Pepsi, and the animals. All of the animals you'll love *and* snow. They've been waiting for us.'

The plane—I realized only now that it was propeller-driven—was dropping quickly through the air. Its rapid descent made me uneasy and slightly ill. I looked out of the window and saw something stunning, electrifying: the airfield was covered with enormous animals—larger than life, larger than even dreams could imagine. From hundreds of feet up, I could see their faces turned towards the sky, towards us. Their eyes, the smallest the size of October pumpkins, were happily expectant. They weren't just waiting for this plane; they were waiting for *us*.

Pepsi was stretched across my lap, his face all wonder and glee.

'And you know all of them, Mommy? You know each one?'

I put one hand on his springy hair and pointed with the other. 'Do you see that big dog there?'

'Yes! He's wearing a hat!'

'Well, that's Mr Tracy. He's the guide.'

'Mr *Tracy?* Cullen, light of my life, only one glass of wine at dinner until the baby comes, okay?'

I looked at my bowl of breakfast food and nodded sheepishly. Danny had a big dumb grin on, but out of pity or something he took my hand across the table.

'Well, maybe you're lucky, Cul. Some people dream about being chased by monsters. At least Yasmuda and Mr Tracy are friends. But you've got to be very careful of dogs wearing hats!'

The dream came and went like the spring breezes. Most nights nothing happened; I dreamed of Danny, or silly unimportant things

36

that had no meaning. One night I dreamt Mr Tracy was putting on a magic show for us and I woke up right after he said, 'Never ask a magician to do his tricks twice. Then they lose all their magic.'

But now and then another episode appeared on my 'dream screen' and by turns I was drawn and repelled by a new world which was growing and filling out before me. I didn't know whether or not it was common for people to have continuous dreams; each night a different but contiguous part of some mysterious whole.

Everything there was unusual, somehow wonderful. The island was named Rondua. The only inhabitants I had seen so far were the big animals: Mr Tracy, Felina the Wolf, Martio the Camel and others. I learned to set my expectations aside and be open to the waves of new stimulus that were forever washing over me. It was a lesson similar to what I had learned in my waking life with Danny, only Rondua was allowed to be and do whatever it pleased because it lived on the other side of sleep, where all bets were off and giant camels spoke Italian.

Danny appeared amused by it for a while, then concerned. He asked me to go to a doctor, which I did. A very spunky *dottore* Anna Zegna told me I was fine and who was my husband to say I shouldn't dream what I wanted? She got so heated about it that I ended up having an argument with her and more or less storming out of her office. No one was going to talk about *my* husband that way!

What I did was keep a notebook about Rondua and what happened when I was there. I kept thinking that what I saw had all the makings of a dandy children's story, but something held me back from writing anything more than a few shorthand notes to myself about the amazing—or the *more* amazing things I encountered. There were times when I even felt frightened by the continally unfolding story, but I rationalized it by saying it was all in some way connected with my pregnancy. I ate candy and I dreamed of my Rondua twice a week. What was so bad about that? I considered myself lucky.

The landscape around the airfield in Rondua was black and surrounded by high black rolling hills. Volcanoes lived here once and had left their mark everywhere.

We stood and watched as the plane started its engines and began to move away. Just as it passed us, the pilot stuck her head out of the window and gave us a big wave.

'Good luck, Pepsi! Cullen, don't forget your book report!'

It was Mrs Eigl, my dreadful sixth-grade teacher. I hadn't seen her fat old face in fifteen years, but I knew it in an instant as one remembers the face of an old nemesis. What the hell was *she* doing here? She even wore one of those old-time leather flying hats with the flaps over both ears, like the Red Baron.

The plane picked up speed and gunned down the black gravel runway. We watched as it lifted up and off and banked hard into the sea-blue sky.

I turned and looked at the funny sad brown face of Martio the Camel.

'Where's that plane going now?'

'To the Happiness of Seals. That's in the south of the Second Stroke.'

'Oh.' I nodded and tried to look as if I knew what he was talking about. Seals? Stroke? Welcome to Rondua!

Mr Tracy and Pepsi were already walking towards a large metal building that looked like a hangar for small planes. I walked fast to catch up, but they had already stopped at the door by the time I reached them.

'Cullen, do you want to tell Pepsi what's inside or should I?'

'Um. Why don't you? I'm still pretty confused.'

'All right.' The dog was so tall that both Pepsi and I had to bend our heads way back to see his face.

'Pepsi, inside here are all the toys your mother owned when she was a girl on the other side. If you'd like, you may have two of them to take along with you on our trip. They have none of the magic of the Bones, but because they were your mother's when she was your age, they may comfort you if you are frightened sometime. Would you like to see them?'

'Oh yeah! What kind of toys?' Pepsi reached for the large door but couldn't pull it, so Felina the Wolf took the clasp carefully in her mouth and did it for him.

There were no windows or electric lights inside, but somehow it was bright as day in there. It took several seconds for the sight to register on me, but when it did, all I could say was, 'Oh, my God!'

On a wooden table in the middle of the hangar were hundreds of toys of all sizes. Immediately I saw the tan stuffed dog with the black nose I had slept with for years when I was a little girl. Every night I would put my arms around it, kiss its nose that squeaked, and say, 'Good night, Farfel.'

'*Farfel!* Where did you get him?'

'We have all of your toys here, Cullen.'

It chilled and excited me—they were a treasured, lost picture album or time capsule. I walked to the table and slowly touched the things I had loved and lost and forgotten; things that had meant the world to me once and now, with a heart-pulling jolt, reminded me of that world. The ballerina I had left in a hotel room in Washington DC, the green sea monster whose yellow tongue popped out when you squeezed him. A 'Winky-Dink' draw-on-your-television-screen kit, a cerise clay statue I had made of my father holding me in his arms: both of us were bald and round and had toothpick holes for eyes, noses and mouths.

Pepsi chose two things I didn't remember at all—a white 'Sky King' cowboy hat and a rubber Popeye doll. It intrigued me to know why *those* two things, but when I asked he shrugged. He wanted to know who Popeye was; he liked the sailor's funny arms.

'He's a guy in cartoons. He eats spinach.'

'What's a cartoon?'

What kid didn't know about cartoons?

On the other hand, what kid was named Pepsi?

I asked Mr Tracy if I could take one of the toys. For some reason, of all the things there, I most wanted to have the small baseball glove I'd used daily one summer when I was six and very much the tomboy. To my surprise, the big dog said a very firm 'No'.

Outside the hangar the sun had just gone down and the sky was the colour of peaches and plums. The wolf and the camel sat waiting for us with two leather knapsacks at their enormous feet. The air smelled of dust and dying heat. The only sounds were those we made.

Pepsi slid on his cowboy hat and carefully adjusted it. We picked up the heavy sacks and started walking north. I *think.*

One night not long after I had this dream, a six-foot nine-inch jerk named DeFazio came down full force on top of Danny in a game and turned his knee into mush. I wasn't there but they told me that, true to form, Danny immediately forgave DeFazio for maiming him.

What followed was the Italian version of a hospital emergency room—*Pronto Soccorso*—where the only pronto thing was complete confusion about what to do about my poor husband's leg.

No one called me, so the first I knew of the disaster was Danny hobbling through our apartment door on a pair of aluminium crutches, his knee taped and bundled . . . and ruined.

I didn't know whether to yell or cry, but I kept my mouth shut because I was afraid either reaction would make Danny feel even worse.

We went through the next few days very carefully, each of us trying to be as kind as possible to the other and not letting them see how very scared we were. I had felt all along that the greatness of the last few months couldn't go on for ever of course, but who is ever prepared for disaster? Life is full of villains and villainous moments, but who wants to think about that? Anyway, what kind of life is it when you are afraid of every knock on the door or every letter in the mailbox?

Danny pretended to take it in his stride, but his worry about what we were going to do next was palpable: his wife was pregnant and his successful career as an athlete was completely *finito*. Life had hit him right in the head with the ball and even sane, calm Danny hadn't a clue about what to do next.

His team paid for the two necessary operations, but then it was, 'Here's your last cheque, pal. See you around.' Their quick, albeit understandable indifference made me livid and made a lot of the days that followed pretty damned dark.

Luckily, by then the season was almost over and we had been planning to visit America anyway. But sitting down one night over the kitchen table, we reviewed everything and decided we would be better off moving back there for good.

We packed everything in a week and said goodbye to a life both of us had grown to like very much. If I had been by myself I would have been in bad shape, but I had Danny James and our baby and I was sorry things had gone wrong, but big deal!

Danny was tremendously cheered by the fact that after making exactly two overseas calls, he landed a job. It was a lovely thing with the New York Parks and Recreational Department, organizing programmes like summer basketball clinics for ghetto kids.

'*Two* phone calls! Danny, if I made two phone calls, one of them would be a wrong number! How on earth did you do it?'

40

He took a coin out of his pocket and 'disappeared' it for me. 'It just happens you're married to a very nice magician, honeybun.'

With the help of my parents, we found our apartment in 'The Axe Boy Arms', as I began calling it after our illustrious downstairs neighbour made his debut. It was on 90th Street near Third Avenue and was a good, sunny place with room enough for both of us as well as the baby when it arrived.

Danny was able to walk normally again by the time we'd moved back and had completely settled into the apartment. But in that time something big had changed in my man. Perhaps it was realizing he too was human—complete with breakable bones, twistable knees, etcetera. He was quieter during those first days back in America and sometimes it was obvious he was brooding, which wasn't like Danny at all. That's not to say he became mean or philosophical or . . . weird. Just a little quieter and more . . . self-contained. Whenever I was able to make him smile or laugh about something, it was one of the day's victories.

The good thing was he liked his job from the start and looked forward to going to work every morning.

We began spending weekends with my parents at their house on Long Island shore. As expected, they loved Danny from the moment they met and the four of us spent good days together, feeling comfortable and eating summer fruit and doing little else besides sitting in the sun and being glad we were all together.

One of the many discoveries I made that summer was realizing I would never again swim in the sea with my father. He was seventy that year and afraid for his heart; a recent operation had left him tired and frightened.

Every year when I was a girl, we spent the entire month of July at my parents' house on the Island. It seemed all we ever did then was swim in the ocean. We had inner tubes, water wings, rafts; a flotilla of things to keep us buoyed up after we'd grown exhausted from doing it with our own limbs.

In my memory, all that remained of those lemony-bright days at the shore were picnic baskets full of beach food—cold fried chicken, lukewarm ginger ale, 'Hostess Snowballs'—and my father's hair plastered down to his head, gleaming, as he swam alongside me in the surf. It was as if he owned the ocean.

My father and I took a lot of walks both when I was a girl and the summer we returned from Europe. My memories of the good old days made him smile and shake his head slowly; the kind of smile you get when you're thinking back to something particularly foolish you did a long time ago. Particularly foolish, but you're glad you did it anyway.

One day he surprised me by touching my stomach gently and familiarly. 'Soon you'll be swimming with your own, eh?'

I smiled and hugged him very hard. He reminded me of Danny in that neither of them showed their emotions much. We kissed when we said hello and goodbye, but that was about it. Sometimes I thought my growing-up had made him shy and uneasy around me. He could touch and kiss and jiggle me on his knee when I was small, but once I grew breasts and started talking to boys on the telephone, I became someone to love and continue to support—but at a distance.

But his operation, and both Danny's disaster and my pregnancy, had brought us closer together. The operation because he had been faced with his own mortality and how everything could disappear in a second; Danny's crushed knee and the coming child because . . . well, maybe because of the same thing. Everything *can* disappear in a second, particularly happiness and structure, but the more you're able to face it square-on, or the more you might even be able to add to the earth that will remain after you've gone, the better. Besides, it would be my father's first grandchild, and I secretly prayed he would live long enough to walk by the sea with this child. Maybe not swim, which was Pop at his best, but at least poke at a few horseshoe crabs together.

Miraculously, Danny and I had landed safely again. I was unused to recoveries like that and it took almost all summer for me to get accustomed to the fact that we were going to be all right after all.

3

Rondua returned. Pepsi and I rode across uninterrupted plains, seated comfortably on the heads of the animals. There were salmon-coloured pyramids in the distance which contrasted sharply with the still-black volcanic ground we passed over.

Felina the Wolf told us the story of her ancestors; of how they rose from the sea as red fish and gave their scales back once they had reached land. It turned out that all of the animals in Rondua had metamorphosed from one species to another when they came here. Clever Pepsi asked if we would have to change too, now that we were here. Mr Tracy, his velvety hat glued to his bobbing head, said we already had.

Martio the Camel often acted as tour-guide, pointing out blue pterodactyls that flew in the distance one morning, telling us to watch closely, another day as the sun began to split in half to mark the end of another Ronduan month.

Many of those early dreams were long, panoramic views of the countryside. There was conversation, but I often lost track of what was being said because I was more interested in what I was seeing. Also, I later realized I paid more attention to the countryside because I already knew many of the stories. Like jokes we hear and then forget until someone begins telling them again, I could have interrupted the animals many times and told my son what came next: how the mountains had learned to run, why only rabbits were allowed pencils, when the birds had decided to become all one colour. This knowledge notwithstanding, I still hadn't a *clue* of why we were in Rondua.

Our first summer back in America moved by with a genial smile on its face and despite New York's torturing heat and humidity, we got used to the pace and once-familiar way of life. It was nice to be able to go to the newest movies that were once again in a language we didn't have to battle to understand. There were book stores and museum exhibits, and once a week my mother and I would sneak off for lunch at one of those expensive restaurants where all the waiters and waitresses were beautiful, but the food tasted the same whether it was supposed to be Turkish or Cantonese.

To my embarrassment, I grew bigger and bigger. I once asked Danny if it were possible to give birth to the Graf Zeppelin. He said it was more likely to be a fourteen-pound Hershey bar.

Sometimes, but only sometimes, I thought about the boy in my dreams and wondered if we would have a son. Then what would I do? Name him Pepsi James? No. We discussed names for the child and decided on 'Walker' for a boy, 'Mae' for a girl. Both of us liked old-fashioned names.

I bought five books on how to bring up a child and so many baby clothes that Danny thought I secretly knew I was due to give birth to triplets, but hadn't told him yet.

On the night of the birth, we watched television until about eleven and then went to bed. A few hours later I woke up, wet and uncomfortable. My water had broken, but both of us were calm and ready as we gathered my bags and headed for the hospital.

The doctor was nice, the labour horrible . . . and the baby came out wailing, red and looking like some kind of live ripe fruit. Mae James. They cleaned her up and put her in my arms for a little while. I was in that euphoria you feel just after a baby is born; right before the pain and exhaustion return in tidal waves. On first glance, she looked pretty tough and spry. Danny appeared out of nowhere and stood on the other side of the room, shy and beaming like a light bulb.

'Come over here, Pop, and see your daughter.'

He started over, his long arms already stretching out for her. Suddenly I felt this tremendous 'whoosh' of fatigue washing over me and I blacked out.

Danny later told me he looked at me at the last moment and luckily guessed I was a breath away from dropping our brand-new child on the floor. He lunged and caught her at the last second.

*

I woke up in Rondua, my head on Pepsi's lap.

'Mommy, you slept so *long!*'

In the dream I *knew* I had just given birth, but I was dressed as before and my body felt fine and fit. I was ready to move on once again. I sat up and looked towards the mountains of Coin and Brick which, if we were lucky, we would be crossing in a few days. Beyond that, I didn't know where we were going. None of the animals were willing to talk about it.

Martio and Felina stood a few feet away, a giant camel and wolf calmly waiting for the sign from us to go. They were so large they blocked out a great deal of the sky from where I was sitting.

'All right, Cullen is awake. Now we can head for the mountains.' Mr Tracy sat nearby, his soft eyes set on the faraway cliffs.

'Is it because of Mae, Mr Tracy? Are we going over there because of the baby?'

'Cullen, you have three questions that you can ask. You've already asked two, and the answers weren't important. They weren't necessary. Your third question may be very helpful to Pepsi later, so be careful.'

He waited for my reply, knowing I wouldn't waste this third, *my* third question on something like this. It seemed like a question that would be answered in time—once we got there, we'd know. I would have to think long and carefully before asking the third.

'Our shortest way is across the plains, but that's also the most dangerous. What should we do?'

The question was addressed to me, and three animals and a little boy waited for my answer.

I looked out across them and could barely make out, flat miles away, the dim but ominous shapes of the Forgotten Machines. Inventions from an age when anything mechanical was considered both positive and magical, they had once easily turned stone into steel; green plants into medicine, cloth, brown fuel. Abandoned later because of failed dreams or newer and better combinations, they had been left to stop and die. But they hadn't. Machines don't die— they wait. Like so many other things in Rondua, they had simply appeared there one day.

Trying to look courageous, I threw back my shoulders and said strongly, 'We've got to go past them. Come on.' I had no idea what I was talking about, but I sensed this was the response they wanted. I walked to Felina and climbed her paw and leg up to her sleek, angled head. I loved that head already, and her yellow wolf eyes both sharp and kind.

When I was growing up, there were three giant cement lions in front of our town library. All of us kids would climb up and over them and never come down until we were either exhausted or their stone coldness had passed into us. I remember loving those lions both for their solidness and size. They were as dependable and permanent as our parents. When I grew older I missed them and my feelings for them.

The Ronduan animals were as large as those lions. But here giant animals spoke and moved and when you climbed on to their backs, their body heat was tropical, often intense. But I felt no fear of them. From the beginning, they were as trustworthy and familiar as the library lions so many years before.

To give us all courage as we moved towards the plains, I began to sing the song of the wooden mice who went to war. I don't know why I remembered it, I didn't even know where it came from, but I certainly knew every word of the song. The others joined in (Pepsi humming after he had listened a while), and we moved a little less apprehensively towards the machines.

'There she is! She's coming round!'

For the first time since the dreams of Rondua began, I woke without really wanting to. I was afraid of what was about to happen to us over there, but also excited and curious. After the gorgeousness and hubbub of this new phase of the Yasmuda dream, waking to my white hospital room—even the new wonder of little Mae—was even at that fortunate time a bit of a letdown.

And then there was so much *pain!* Mae had decided to enter the world feet-first. Consequently, with all the pushing and pulling and turning they did before she actually made the scene, a good part of my lower innards was a disaster area.

Some time later, the doctor said he had had to put fifty stitches in me just to repair the damage. For days afterwards I walked around bowlegged and slow and *very* carefully, reminding myself of those pictures of astronauts on the moon, walking through weightlessness. Except that those guys got to bounce from here to there in big cartoony leaps. Whenever I stepped wrongly, every pain bell in my system went off with a jangle.

Needless to say I wasn't at my best, but Danny treated me marvellously. He brought flowers and candy and a pair of green velvet bedroom slippers so ugly that they made me cry for love of him.

In between all this, I would hobble slowly down the hall to see the baby. I'd hobble back to my room a few minutes later, astounded that she was still there. She actually existed and was ours!

A cloud over all of this nice sky was remembering one night in bed that the last time I had been in a hospital was when I had had the abortion. I looked at the black ceiling above me and said a prayer for everyone—Mae, Danny, the dead child, myself, my parents. Saying the prayer didn't make me feel any better, but the words alone were soothing company and they helped me to sleep. I remember dreaming that night of magicians with giant hands making babies appear and disappear like the coins in Danny's tricks.

I didn't dream of Rondua again until a few days after Mae and I went home. That's where it all began.

It began. Yes, *it* began on one of those mornings when everyone you pass on the street seems to be wearing nice cologne.

October is a temperamental month in New York. It can be as courtly as Fred Astaire or as surly and mean as a summons server. It was on its best behaviour the first week we were back, but then it turned. I spent hour after quiet hour by the window in a rocking-chair, feeding Mae, watching the first hard rains fall.

You can lose yourself watching rain as easily as you can watching a fire. Both are deliberate yet whimsical, completely engrossing in no time at all.

After Danny left for work, I would cart Mae and a white blanket over to the window in the living-room, plop us down in the chair with the blanket over both of us, and settle in for my daily ration of rain watching. She would slurp her breakfast while I watched the silvery-blue, wet windows lighten as the day came to earth. The rain swept and blew back and forth angrily, but I liked it and felt protected by it.

One morning the clouds cracked open and the sun slipped through like a big yellow egg-yolk. It decided to stay around for a while too. By that time I had fallen into such a state of sitting and gazing that the gleam and bright snap of yellow everywhere made me sit right straight up—as if someone had clapped their hands behind my head.

I bustled around the apartment getting ready and had us out on

47

the glistening street in no time. Mae wore a peach-coloured suit and appeared very pleased by the change of surroundings.

'Hi, Mrs James. Strange weather, huh?'

Alvin Williams came out of the door behind me and started talking before I'd even turned round. His voice sounded friendly enough, but when I turned to look at him there was no expression on his face. He might just as well have been looking at a door.

'Hi, Alvin! Where's Loopy?'

'He's a pain sometimes. I wanted to go out by myself and look at these clouds. Will you look at those colours! It's like they're having a fist-fight or something up there, huh?'

I liked that image and smiled at him without looking at the sky. I knew what he was talking about, but Alvin Williams with his dirty glasses and Buddy Holly haircut didn't seem the kind of fellow who would come up with images like that.

'Well, Alvin, this is an historic day for us. This is the first time Mae James here has ever gone for a walk.'

He smiled and looked into the carriage. 'Is that right? Well, congratulations. You and Mr James should have champagne or something tonight to celebrate.'

We chatted for a few more minutes, but then he became sort of nervous and said he had to go. That was okay with me, because I wanted to get moving.

'So now! Welcome to 90th Street, Mae. There's the market where I shop for us. Over there is the book-store your Daddy likes . . .'

I gave her the quick guided tour of our neighbourhood and besides Alvin, everybody *did* smell of good cologne.

It still hurt me to walk much, so I stopped after fifteen minutes in front of Marinucci's Ice Cream Emporium—a favourite watering-hole of the James family. I went in and ordered coffee and checked to see if Mae was still tucked up tight in the right places.

A waitress I had never seen before brought the coffee to my table and didn't even peek at the baby.

'Cretin.' I picked up the cup and made a face at her retreating back. The cup wasn't hot and the coffee was barely warm when I sipped it.

I clunked it back down on the table and looked out of the window. I hate lukewarm coffee. It has to be hot, *hot;* almost enough to burn your tongue. The waitress was reading a magazine at the counter and I was about to call her over and complain when I looked at the mug. Steam swirled up from it and carried the good smell of fresh ground coffee in it.

Huh? I touched it to be sure. *Hot.* Hormones? It must have been hormones, or my body, or something inside readjusting or calibrating after the shock of the birth. Or else I had become so stoned looking out of the window at grey and blue rain that I'd grown dull or wobbly or even just *off* about certain things; things like heat and time and memory.

Shrugging it off, I picked up the cup and blew over it to cool it. It was so hot I could barely keep my finger crooked through the ceramic hole. Hey Danny, guess what happened to me today? I shook my head, knowing I wouldn't tell him about this because it would make me look very silly.

So I had my coffee, paid and left. Passing the window on the way home again, I glanced in at the table where I'd sat, but the cup was gone. Funny.

As we approached across the plains of Rondua, the sound of the forgotten machines became gigantic, oiled and precise. I began to make out their separate parts: pistons and levers moving in a glistening storm of chrome, brass and tight compression. They no longer *made* anything, but continued to function. The ground they sat on was theirs, inviolable to others.

When we were within a few hundred feet of the first one, it slowed suddenly like an old steam locomotive coming into a station. On its side was a large red and gold plaque that said 'Lieslseiler: Prague'. Its separate pieces slackened down to half-speed, although it hissed and clanked even more than before. I was sure it had somehow sensed our presence. Its message and then its pace was quickly —frighteningly—picked up by the other machines. As one, they worked down to the same rhythm, despite each being entirely different from the other.

I felt the wolf's body tremble beside me and I knew it was my place to speak.

'Let us through. You know who we are. We're not your enemies. We have to cross the plains and then the mountains.'

The machines mocked me by clacking their levers up and down in perfect time to my last words. When I stopped, they went back to their own mysterious rhythms.

'Leave us alone.'

Clack-Clack-Clack-Clack.

Together, they sounded like the largest typewriter in the world. I looked at Martio, but his round camel's face gave no hint as to what to do.

'Please, just *stop.*'

Clack-Clack-Clack.

Minutes passed. Their movements and pace stayed the same so long as no one spoke, while their steam whistled savagely up into the dry air.

'They want the word, Cullen.'

I looked at Mr Tracy, shocked that he had even mentioned it here in front of the others, in front of the machines! But they had remained silent after he spoke.

Pepsi had his arms wrapped around the wolf's front leg and his face was scared. He looked at me as if *I* knew what to do.

'But why, Mr Tracy?'

'Because it's the only proof of who you are. It proves why you're here.'

'But won't we need it later?'

The machines' tempo quickened; they were offended by my hesitation.

'You need it now. Use it!' Mr Tracy's voice was quiet but firm. I had no choice.

'Koukounaries!'

They stopped.

An hour later, the wolf came up alongside and Pepsi broke the sullen silence which had been with us since we passed so quickly and anxiously across the rest of the Plain of Machines.

'Mom, what does it mean? Koucarry?'

I looked at Mr Tracy; he was a few feet ahead of us but he had turned when he heard the boy's question. He nodded for me to answer. It was the first magic I ever gave my son.

'Koukounaries, Pepsi. It means *pine cones* in Greek.'

The doctor's name was Rottensteiner and his office was decorated with cheerful photographs of his family and their Golden Retriever dogs.

I sat in a chair across the desk from him and told him the whole story of my Rondua dreams. It made me nervous to be spilling these same beans again for the second time in a year, once on each side of the ocean, but the Koukounaries dream had scared me. I wanted to get this whole thing out of my system, or at least find an angle on it that I could accept and live with.

When I had finished, he steepled his fingers and shrugged. 'I honestly don't think anything is wrong, Mrs James. I've never heard of this happening before, but that's nothing new in this field. Your doctor in Italy was right, so far as I can tell. Dreams do what they want. You can't put a leash on them and tell them where to walk.

'People usually have repetitious or sequential dreams after some kind of traumatic experience—they've been in a bad car accident, or someone they loved recently died—something bad that the system just can't let go of. Now, the fact that you seem to be both happy and well-adjusted tells me that you're dreaming of Rondua because a part of you enjoys it. Nothing more or less. To tell you the God's-honest truth, I don't *know* why it has gone on for so long, or why it's so clearly episodic. But as a doctor, that doesn't make me concerned. Obviously the most recognizable thing is that you're incorporating parts of your conscious world into Rondua. The Greek pine cones is the best example. Why? I don't know. For some reason, your subconscious has decided to use that particular bit because it likes it. It *is* a strange word, but there's no rhyme or reason for how that part of the mind works. It's both a stubborn and a mysterious thing and it really does end up doing or thinking exactly what it pleases.'

'And I shouldn't worry?'

'Of course you could come and talk to me once a week about your life and what may be on your mind that day. But I would be cheating you. You sound fine, from what you've told me. You like your husband, you're enjoying your child . . . To me, your life sounds like its moving along in high gear. If anything bad does come of the dream eventually, then by all means come back here and we'll talk. But I don't think that will happen. If I were you, I'd let Rondua do what it wants. Maybe if you really dislike it, the less you resist it, the more apt it will be to go away.'

I was a greenhorn in the land of psychiatry and psychology, so having heard the same judgement from two doctors, I slid the 'Am-I-mad?' worries to the back burner of my overactive mind.

Danny knew nothing of my visit to Rottensteiner, or the fact that the Rondua dreams had been continuing. But some weeks after I had returned from the hospital, he did ask how Yasmuda and the gang were doing.

51

I handed him a wet child and refused to look at him. He took Mae, but stood there waiting for my answer. He was concerned and that concern invariably made me want to hug him. I told him I still dreamt about Rondua once in a while, but nothing like before. He asked if that made me *sad,* which I thought was a queer question, coming from him.

'Sad? Weren't you the one who was so worried when I was having them before?'

'Yeah, I was, Cul. But it's just that you seemed . . . really happy when you dreamed of them. I even liked hearing what was happening in the next exciting adventure: Felina the Wolf; Mr Tracy, the dog with the hat on . . .'

'You remember them?'

'How could I forget?'

The real winter days came and things grew cold and blue and very still.

Being a mother was much harder and more monotonous than I had originally imagined. In my pre-Mae musings, I had envisioned days pleasantly full of pragmatic duties that led to a smiling, happy baby and my feeling worthy for a series of small jobs well done. But there was always so much *to* do, and it had to be done over and over again. Things were only complete for a moment. As soon as you turned your back or closed your eyes for a second, the bottles were all dirty again and the nappy needed changing, and what about that load of laundry you put in an hour ago? Mae was a very good kid and fussed only when she had reason to, but there were a lot of reasons and sometimes her fussing made me short-tempered and frustrated as hell.

And then I always tried to have our small world all shipshape and spic and span by the time Danny came home from work in the evening. It was important to me that he shouldn't walk into the kind of mess some friends of ours allowed because of their kids. I recoiled at the idea of toys everywhere, chocolatey faces, that repugnant smell of cooped-up child I knew from visits to other houses.

Maybe down-deep I wanted Danny to think I was Wonderwoman in every conceivable way. Attractive, bright, sexy as the devil, but most of all—competent. We want to be loved for what we are, but also for what we want others to *think* we are.

Weekends were best, because Danny was around to pitch in and help out with the washing and the shopping. Sometimes we'd arrange for a babysitter and go out to dinner and a movie. It was a big help and what was nicest about those breaks was that we'd both come home renewed and excited to see the baby again.

It snowed all the time. It was too cold to go out most days and too warm in the apartment. One particularly gloomy afternoon, I sat with Mae on my lap and felt suddenly that if I didn't find something to do fast the walls were going to eat me. I had not dreamed of Rondua for a while, which was too bad because it would have given me something to think about during the endless feedings. As an exercise while sitting there, I tried to remember the finer details of what I had seen and experienced: the mysterious colour combinations, the way amber light fell across the Ronduan mountains at daybreak and sunset.

Remembering daily life is difficult enough, God knows. Remembering dreams days or even months later is a wee bit more difficult.

When Mae had had her fill and dozed off, I put her in her crib. Rummaging around in a desk drawer, I dug up the notebook I had kept when the first dreams started. I hadn't put anything in the book since our return to America months before, but this time I set to work putting down these newest Ronduan scenes before they slipped away from me completely. The more I wrote, the more I remembered: the colour of the camel's eyes, the sound of Felina's leathery feet padding across sandy ground.

My mind, which since Mae's birth had fallen into a kind of sleepy stupor, stretched and began shaking other parts of itself awake. It was like 'Reveille' played in an Army barracks; one guy got up, then another, and soon the whole place was clattery noise and blankets thrown aside, feet hitting the floor everywhere.

I filled a few sides without worrying whether it was sequential or chronological or logical. It was a diary and diaries are conversations with yourself. *I* understood what I was trying to say, so it didn't matter whether the entries made perfect sense or not.

The hours didn't 'fly by', but I did spend a long afternoon at it, working myself into a kind of tiredness I hadn't known for a long time—the kind of tiredness that comes at the end of good hard work which means something to you.

When Danny came home I was very animated and glad to see him. I didn't say anything about the notes, because I wanted to think about why I was really writing them. Were they catharsis, or just a way of passing time? Perhaps I was even laying the ground-work for the children's book I had thought about writing earlier. I didn't know what was at the heart of this and until I did, I decided to keep it all quiet.

A few days later I bought a very sharp leather notebook at a stationery store and started transferring everything into it. I knew I was getting serious when I forked out twenty-seven dollars for a notebook: I hadn't kept a real one since college. I was both stirred and intimidated by the vast number of unfriendly white pages in there. I don't have very nice handwriting, so I wrote slowly and very carefully, enjoying the act in itself and understanding for the first time why monks had once devoted so much time to illuminating manuscripts.

The first thing I tried to do in that pretty book was pull all my Yasmuda dreams together and somehow shape them up. I began with the first dream and my first words to Pepsi when we were in the plane, descending on Rondua.

'I remember when the sea was full of fish with mysterious names; Mudrake, Cornsweat, Yasmuda, and there wasn't much to do in a day.'

While Mae slept or lay in her bassinet, eyeing her pink owl mo-bile, I wrote.

4

My mother took Mae and me out for lunch to 'Amy and Joe's': one of those presumptuous 'really American' restaurants where they served us okay chili for seven dollars a bowl.

Walking home through breezy cold, Mom insisted on pushing the baby carriage the whole way. She talked about how one day all three of us girls would be having lunch together. Her face was one big smile after she said that.

The thought intrigued me. What would Mae James be like when she was old enough to sit at a restaurant table, legs long enough for her feet to touch the floor, her face interesting enough to draw the looks of men?

'What are you thinking about, dear?'

'About how kids get gypped by their parents. Their birth is *our* second beginning, but then our death is the beginning of their end.'

'That's very poetic, but don't be morbid, dear: it's bad for the complexion. Isn't that your building? What's going on down there?'

Alarmingly, five police cars stood at strange angles to the kerb in front of our apartment house. The drivers had been in too great a hurry to worry about proper parking.

Thank God in heaven I knew Danny was safe at work. I had called ten minutes before to warn him that dinner would be late due to 'lunch-with-Mom'.

'Cullen, it looks like something bad has happened. Should you come over to our apartment? We'll get a cab and call Danny from there.'

'No, Mom, I want to see what's happened. It could have something to do with our apartment. Maybe I didn't turn the gas off . . .'

55

We came to the barriers the police had put up to keep people back.

'Officer, I live here. What's happening?'

'Had a couple of murders, lady. Some nut killed his mother and sister. Somethin' real bad.'

People like to say that immediately after they heard the news they knew who did it, but I'd be lying if I said that. At the moment, I didn't even remember Alvin Williams *lived* in the building. He wasn't the most memorable guy you'll ever meet, apart from his crimes.

'Holy shit, look at that damned guy!'

We had been chatting with the policeman, who knew nothing more about what had happened. He was the first to see that they were bringing Alvin out of the house. It was the middle of the day, but he wore a plaid pyjama top over what I *think* was a skirt. I couldn't tell because I was too shocked, then too drawn by the expression on his familiar face. Calm: absolute and total calm. His hands were handcuffed in front of him and he kept stumbling as he walked out of the building to the first police car.

'Look at the fuckin' blood, man!'

Two black teenagers in identical windbreakers and green watch caps stood next to us, taking everything in.

'He musta fuckin' cut the shit out of evvabody *in* there.'

'Mother *fucker*, man! Where's his knife at?'

'Cullen, come on. Let's go to our house.'

We had started back from the barriers when Alvin shouted, 'Mrs James! Hey!'

His excited hoot grabbed me like a lasso and I froze where I was, but couldn't get up the nerve to turn and look at him.

'How're you, Mrs James! How's the baby!'

A man in a ski jacket came up to me and showed his police badge. He was a nice-looking man. I heard doors close behind me, a siren start its wail.

'Do you mind if I talk to you for a minute, lady?'

'Want to know something strange? One of the last times I ever talked to Alvin, I came in here afterwards for a cup of coffee.'

We were sitting in Marinucci's Ice Cream Emporium. The police detective's name was Gabe Flossmann and he had a soft voice wrapped around a thick New York accent.

56

'How well did you know him, Mrs James? Did you ever have him over or anything, or go to his place?'

I shivered involuntarily. 'No, nothing like that. We were just hall-friends, you know what I mean? "Hello, good morning. How's your dog?" Nothing beyond that.'

'And you say the dog's name was *Loopy?*' He looked at the pad in his hand. I'd been surprised at how much he'd written down so far.

I nodded, then turned my head from side to side to ease the tension-knot which sat in the middle of my neck.

Flossmann put down his pencil and looked out of the window. 'I tell ya, Mrs James, this city's become a real bees' nest of crazies. When I first joined the force twelve years ago, you'd have some lunatic doing something like this maybe once every few months or so. Then you throw in a few horrors from the Mafia and you'd get— I don't know—maybe ten or twelve really bad murders in a year. But *now*, hell, it's like every night some bongo goes bananas and every night it's something else. Last week, down on 84th Street? Some woman got mad at her baby and crucified the poor thing on the bathroom door! I mean, can you imagine? That takes a big imagination, right? And you know what else? She must have had ten different crucifixes up in that apartment. Gold ones, ones that lit up . . . How do they think these things up?'

Horribly, I couldn't stop my mind from flashing a picture of Mae crucified on a wall in our apartment. My heart started beating really hard in my chest. I closed my eyes and told myself to stop it. Taking very deep breaths, I squeezed my hands together and looked at Flossmann.

'What will happen to Alvin now?'

'He'll be arraigned and they'll get him a lawyer and then probably send him over to Bellevue for observation. Are you okay, Mrs James? You're looking a little queasy.'

A week later Danny was watching a Formula One car race on television. I was puttering around the apartment accompanied by the too-loud snarl of car engines from the set.

Coming in from the kitchen, I had a direct view of the TV when one of the cars—driven by a Colombian named Pedro Lopez—flew off the road, hit a wall and exploded.

I froze in the doorway, unable to look away from the blaze or the burning pieces of racing car flying up and scattering all over the track.

'He's a goner.' Danny said it in his quietest, saddest voice.

There was great courage shown in those next few minutes. Men, some in fireproof suits and some just wearing shorts and teeshirts, came running towards the fire. They completely disregarded the soaring flames and the danger that was everywhere. Some of them had fire extinguishers, others nothing but their hands and hope. They fought the flames, fought through them to the hapless man still visible but completely motionless in what was left of the cockpit of his car.

The commentator tried to be calm, but the sight of the poor driver burning to death made even the professional's voice quaver and finally drop to almost a whisper.

After a few seconds, I realized I was standing there saying to myself, 'Don't die. Don't die.'

They finally killed the fire with extinguishers that blew chemical smoke everywhere and coated everything a chalky, dead white. A helicopter landed on the track and attendants ran out with a stretcher and medical bags.

'Don't die. Don't die.' It was a litany; an incantation only I heard. I'm sure of that, because Danny never turned round the whole time I was saying it.

The announcer said that Lopez was twenty-four and this was his first season driving a Formula One car. They eased him out of the wreck, laid him on a blue stretcher and flew him away to the hospital.

Danny turned off the television and we waited there in its cooling, disappearing glow for something we knew was impossible: the man's life to continue.

On the news that night, the sports announcer talked about the race and showed replays of the accident too many times. They showed a smiling picture of Lopez and said he was still alive, although in very critical condition. It was a miracle he had survived that long and the doctors were not at all optimistic about his chances.

When I got into bed I prayed for him. I have said the Lord's Prayer every night for years before I go to sleep, but I rarely pray for anyone or anything in particular. I'm convinced God exists, but he doesn't need us to tell him how to run his show. He knows. But this time I asked that Lopez be allowed to live.

In the Rondua dream that followed, all of us stood at the base of a mountain, staring unbelievingly at a small dead-white thing that looked like a piece of driftwood. Mr Tracy turned to me and spoke in a barely restrained, excited voice.

'You were right, Cullen, there it is! Go and pick it up.'

'What is it, Mommy?' Pepsi's voice, behind me and suddenly very far away, sounded scared.

Without answering him I moved forward, stooped and picked it up. It was heavy and solid—not any kind of wood at all. I turned to the others and held it out towards them with both hands.

'It's a bone, sweetheart. One of the Bones of the Moon.'

I felt nothing special, nothing different. I knew what it represented, but I held and regarded it as something that made little difference.

Felina, surprising us all, let out a cry that was half wolf snarl, half jubilant bark. It echoed up across the mountain and sent a gigantic flock of metal birds racketing off their perches, out on to the plains we had just crossed.

Mr Tracy and I looked at each other and he smiled and nodded his approval. This was why I had returned to Rondua—to help them find the first Bone of the Moon. I knew that now, but I knew nothing else. I looked at the bone and had a terrible urge to throw it as far away from me as I could. The longer I held it, the more I realized what it was and how strong it could be. It had taught me magical words, had once given me magical powers I neither wanted nor understood. It had almost killed me. I remembered that too. The Bones meant too much and I doubted again, after so many years, if anyone was capable of controlling them.

'What *is* it, Mommy?' My son looked at me, uncomprehending and still very afraid. Only now his fear had moved from the puzzling thing in my hand to me. He was too young to understand what it all meant, and I was incapable of explaining it to him. I was also very afraid for all of us, but I didn't know why. I felt like an animal, like a bird which suddenly feels the violent urge to fly out to sea. An earthquake is coming, but birds don't have words like that in their vocabulary—only the mysterious good sense to know things are about to go wrong and it's time to leave.

59

*

Bees the size of coffee cans flew silently over the river. It was dusk and the water had abandoned the light. The colour of brown leather, it moved sluggishly, as if something was holding back its flow.

I took Pepsi's hand and led him down to the shore.

'Look hard and you'll see the fish in there, Pepsi. Tonight we'll all swim together with them.'

It was too dark to see through the deep flow. I didn't want him to be frightened, but I had forgotten children's willingness to accept anything, so long as it is wonderful. The thought of a night swim with mysterious, unknown fish was heaven to him; his small features beamed.

I undressed and left my clothes where they fell. Pepsi was in such a hurry that in two seconds he was a tangle of sleeves and pants in an angry knot at his ankles.

The animals waited until I had freed him and we were ready. Then they walked first into the water. I held Pepsi's hand and followed Martio's high hump. The water was cold but not uncomfortable. I felt the first smooth mud beneath my feet, between my toes. Pepsi squeezed my hand tight when the first shock of cold ran through his body.

The fish rose as one to meet us. Their shapes and colours were impossible to describe. You could say that this one looked like a headlight with eyes, that one like a key with fins, but it would be pointless.

We dived deep and were able to stay under as long as we pleased —Pepsi too, who earlier had said he didn't know what 'swimming' was.

The animals stayed near and let us ride on their backs for great long distances. We raced and dived and made fast, sharp turns back to where we'd started. I clung to the wolf's warm fur and watched fish slip and glide across each other's phosphorescent paths. Water comets, they grouped and fled and returned to us.

When we had been under a long time, Mr Tracy swam to me with the first Bone in his teeth. It was very warm when I took it from him. Holding either end, I pushed down and the thing snapped easily in half. I felt a charge of energy or power go up either arm, like bubbles in a glass of ginger ale. Halved, the two pieces were much lighter in my hands. On land, it had been rock-heavy and

60

hard, but here in the water—the only place where the moon held sway—the Bone could and *had* to be broken for us to succeed.

I swam to Pepsi and gestured for him to take one half. When he did, I swam a little away, then turned and faced him again. I held up my piece and nodded for him to do the same. When both our arms were up over our heads, an arc of purple light floated easily between the two parts of the Bone. There was no sound at all, no Van de Graf generator snapping static white electricity from one ground to the other. Between the pieces of bone, only a soft arcing purple light swam silently. It was very beautiful and not frightening at all.

Later we dried off in our clothes and sat by a fire Felina had brought from miles away. The dog gave me two knives of obsidian and I handed one to Pepsi. He took it and stabbed it into the earth a few times.

'Pepsi, tonight we're going to make our walking sticks with these pieces of bone. Watch me and you'll see how to do it.'

The animals retreated back into the darkness and we set to work carving the Bones of the Moon. Now and then I looked towards the water and saw that all the fish were near, watching us from just beneath the surface. Their eyes glowed.

Pepsi watched and learned three lifetimes' worth of carving in a few hours. Leaves and ocelots, a little man who looked like Alvin Williams, a woman's upturned hand filled with stones and frogs . . . These figures and more wound up and around the pale, crooked sticks and ended up all entering the moon's broken face.

The camp-fire light flickered yellow and orange across our busy hands. I kept looking up to see if Pepsi was doing it right, to make sure he didn't cut himself. My heart jumped like a dolphin in my chest to see his little boy's face so tight with concentration and concern. The sharp wrinkles that were only visiting now would someday own his face and he would be a man. We would talk intelligently then and I would be the one to ask too many questions and want his constant attention. I loved knowing he would be a man. I hated knowing the boy would disappear into photograph albums and small worn-out blue jeans that ended up as window-cleaning rags.

He was finishing the figure of a racing car when he felt either my gaze or my sadness. Looking up abruptly, he asked if he could lick his stick when we were finished.

'Why would you want to do *that?*'

61

'Because it looks like it'll taste good.'

I laughed and said yes and felt better. He wasn't a man yet!

The racing driver Lopez lived. I found an article in the newspaper which said he was burned everywhere and that they were keeping him plugged in to all kinds of machinery while he slept on in a deep coma. But he lived. I kept thinking of the racing cars we had carved on our sticks in Rondua.

One afternoon, sitting by the window with Mae, I envisioned a figure in a bed wrapped like a mummy. The only sounds around it were the jitter and hum of life-support systems. It was death in life and I knew who it was and it made me shiver uncontrollably. I thought of Lopez's family; their present pain and impossible hopes for the future. Would he continue to live for years, always at the mercy of transparent tubes and yellow dials which marked smooth brain-waves and a change in body temperature of one degree?

I thought of my husband Danny and tried to imagine how I would feel if he were Lopez and his life was being kept on only by imperceptible electric currents which entered his body every few seconds. Life was certainly precious, but death even more so in some cases. In the quietest whisper, I said, 'Let him die.'

He died the next morning.

5

Eliot Kilbertus and I became great pals because we kept bumping into each other in the basement laundry room. One look at him told you he was as gay as Dick's hatband. He'd often arch his left eyebrow up into his scalp and his hands did little fan dances when he spoke to you—but oh, how he spoke!

'I have been *spying* on you and your husband ever since you moved in, you know. You're Cullen James, right? I'm Eliot Kilbertus. Actually, my real name is Clayton *Drury*, but I changed it when I was seven. I mean, Drury-Dreary, right? I refuse to go through my life sounding like a Dickens character. Where did you get that sweater?'

'Bloomingdale's.'

'I thought so. You should buy only Italians, honey. They *last.*'

'Could you move over a little, Eliot? I can't see my dryer.'

That first day we talked, he was so 'on' that I thought he was trying out for a part in some show and had mistaken me for the casting director. He didn't stop for a minute and his monologue ranged from the genius of Italian designers to his pug dog, Zampano, who was at the time suffering from the flu.

'Of course dogs get flu, Cullen. Are you mad? Imagine walking down the sidewalks of New York in bare feet. What you'd pick up! AIDS galore. Plague Paradise, *kinder.* Would you like to come up to my apartment after we're done here? I've only got one more rinse. Your daughter is extremely quiet, Cullen. Is she dead?'

His place was campy and fun. He wrote film reviews for one of the gay New York newspapers and his walls were covered with posters of terrible films like *Attack of the Killer Tomatoes* and *Senior Prom.*

He made delicious cappucino in one of those ornate silver Gaggia

63

machines I'd seen so often in the expresso bars in Italy. Then he picked up one of his dog's squeaky toys and after giving it a thorough washing in the sink, held it over Mae's travelling bed and squeezed it until she started to cry.

'Well, I mean, what do you want, honey? I'm not Captain Kangaroo!'

'I think she hates that, Eliot. But thanks for trying.'

He calmed down over the course of the afternoon and was speaking normally by the time I looked at my watch and realized how late it was. We made a date for lunch together the next day and I went home feeling good.

Danny liked him too. The first time Eliot came over for dinner, he was surprisingly shy and on his best behaviour. For a while. Once he saw how nice and unjudgemental my husband was, he fired right up again and had us giggling all through the spinach lasagne.

'Oh Cullen, you really *are* a vegetarian! I just thought you were slim. But you must give Mae meat, though; I'm totally serious about that. My friend Roger Waterman was brought up vegetarian and he turned into an accountant!'

In between the exclamation points and cunning remarks, Eliot Kilbertus was a considerate, overly-generous man. He worked at home most of the time and would often call up and ask if I would like him to babysit for a while so that I could go out and do things. Sometimes I took him up on the offer because it was genuine and not an 'I'll do you a favour *IF* you'll do me one' sort of thing. He liked us and we liked him and we began spending more and more time together.

When we got to know each other better, he admitted he was wealthy because he was an only child and his parents had been in Florida real estate before they died. They had left him 'great skads' of money which he had invested carefully and successfully. Every time he came to dinner he brought some kind of extravagant wine or bread or pâté that didn't have anything to do with what I was serving but tasted good anyhow.

He always dressed in beautiful clothes, which he bought on semiannual trips to Europe where he 'went mad buying and eating and doing'. When he heard that we had lived for a year in Italy, he shook his head and told us we were retarded to have ever moved back to the United States of McDonald's. When Danny asked Eliot why *he* didn't live over there, he shrugged and said he couldn't read

64

Italian movie magazines and none of the drug stores sold dental floss.

When the weather was okay, we'd go out walking with Mae in her carriage and the two of us on either side. Then another side of Eliot showed itself. I soon realized he *couldn't* have lived anywhere but New York, because it was one of the few things he really loved. A walk with him meant an ongoing lecture about architecture, Frederick Law Olmstead's original plans for Central Park and where the best walnut brownies in the city could be found.

He took us to gallery openings and to a concert in Soho where thirty-two people listened to six people snip the air with scissors, all thirty-eight of us wearing totally serious expressions on our faces. It was a hoot; both Danny and I loved it. When the concert was over, Danny slipped into a dime store and bought three pairs of those silver, round-ended scissors like you had in kindergarten.

'Let's go home and do an encore!'

Wednesday afternoons Eliot and I got into the habit of having lunch together in our apartment. He'd eat a meatball wedge or a souvlaki gyro, while I polished off hunks of feta cheese and black Greek olives or spaghetti al burro. When we were done, we would settle down for a couple of hours of gab.

That's how I found out about his interest in the occult. He told me about a party he'd gone to where they had used a ouija board to summon the ghost of Amelia Earhart. I rolled my eyes at that and asked if she had flown into the room. That made him very mad. He believed wholeheartedly in 'other powers' and was offended when I joked about the subject. It was one of the only times he ever got mad at me.

'You're such a little wise guy, Cullen. Let me see your hand.'

Rondua galloped across my mind and I felt uneasy about letting him have a look.

'Oh come on, Cullen. I'm not asking you to undress. Just let me look at your hand; I want to see what's up with you.'

I knew the left hand was what you're born with and the right is what you've done with it. I didn't know which would be more revealing to let him see.

'No, give me your right hand. Okay, let's see what we have here.'

He didn't take one look and jump in the air which, after my recent Rondua dreams, I was half-expecting. He squeezed the pads

65

of my palm and fingers, then turned the hand over and back a few times.

'Well, my dear, I'm afraid you are very uninteresting, palm-wise. It says you'll be happily married, your children will turn out okay and you'll live longer than I will.'

'Seriously, Eliot, do you believe in occult things?'

His face said yes before he did. 'Without any question, Cullen. I've seen too many things *not* to believe it.'

'Then will you promise not to tell anyone if I tell you something? Especially not Danny?'

'Cross my heart, Mrs James.'

I took a deep, deep breath and for the fourth time in one year, launched into the story of Rondua.

Eliot chewed his lip and looked at his fingernails while I spoke, but I knew he was paying attention.

'And Danny knows all about it?'

'All but the recent parts. Not about the racing driver and Alvin Williams being in there too. It worried him enough before; he thought something was going wrong with me.'

'But the shrinks said you were all right, right? Not that those dunces know what they're talking about! I once went to a psychiatrist who told me I'd get better if I painted my apartment green.'

'No, both of them said it was a little *abnormal* for the dreams to go on in such perfect . . . order, but it was nothing to really worry about.'

We dropped the subject a while later when Mae woke from her nap and started complaining. But later that evening, he called and said he had talked with a friend of his who owned a book-store. This friend was a big Doris Lessing fan and she had once told Eliot something about Lessing that rang a bell in his head when we talked.

'Cullen, you're insane, but you're not at *all* original. According to my friend Elisabeth Zobel, Doris Lessing has what she calls "serial dreams". Here, listen to this: it's a quote from an interview Doris did in London: "I had serial dreams. I don't mean to say necessarily the same story. But when I have a certain dream, I know it is the same area of my mind . . . But it is not like a film which ends at a certain place or event. What happens is, I dream in the same area, like the same landscape or the same people, but above all the same feeling, the same atmosphere." '

I closed my eyes and sighed a big deep sigh. It sounded so familiar.

'It sounds similar, Eliot, but not exactly the same.' I looked around
the room to make sure Danny wasn't within earshot. 'How come
Alvin Williams and that racing driver were in there too?'

'Because they're part of your *life*, dumbie! Cullen, I'll bet you a
million dollars Doris Lessing has her Alvin Williams too. All of us
take things from our everyday life and stick them right in our
dreams—and usually crookedly too. You and Doris make a lovely
pair. Good night, Mrs Norman Bates. Say hello to your husband for
me.'

Early one morning we came up over a soft rise and below us, a mile
or two away, was a wide paved road that stretched all the way to
the horizon.

I was sitting on top of Martio's high hump, holding Pepsi in front
of me. Mr Tracy stood next to us, our Bones of the Moon walking
sticks stuck in the black silk band of his enormous hat.

'Should I know about that road, Mr Tracy?'

'No, I don't think so, Cullen. It was built after you left. Some of
the machines on the plain just started up and began working on it.
They kept at it until they had made a road that crosses all of
Rondua. None of us know what it's for, but it does get you places
twice as fast. If you want to go and visit Jackie Billows in the Conversation Bath some day, just get on that road and you'll be there a
week earlier than you first planned.'

'Well, does anyone ever use it?'

'Not that I know of.' He stopped and looked at Martio and Felina,
who both shook their heads.

Martio raised his head and turned to face us as best he could
around his hump. 'Once in a while they'll have a party on it, de-
pending on which Stroke you're in. It's a very good surface to dance
on.'

Although we were far from the road, I could see something moving towards us from the horizon very quickly.

'Look, there's something coming our way!'

'Yeah, look, Mom! What's that, Mr Tracy?'

'That? That's just the speed of sound. Sometimes, if you're very
lucky, you'll be able to see the speed of light go by too, but that's
rare. Sizzling Thumb likes to keep as much light as he can in his

Stroke. But the speed of sound is so common, and there's so much *of* it . . . Most of us just ignore it if we're near. If you wait a minute, you'll hear it and know what I mean.'

The sound from the road arrived a few seconds later. It was the noise I had known all of my life—cars, whistles, people talking, footsteps—everything smashed together in a big bunch. For a moment, the air around us was thick with it, but it passed.

Pepsi turned and looked at Mr Tracy, his small face serious and adult. 'Where are we going now, Mr Tracy?'

'We have to find the second Bone, Pepsi. *You* have to find it. And before that, we have to go and meet Sizzling Thumb. Do you remember him, Cullen?'

The boy and the three animals looked at me. I felt so stupid looking back and shaking my head. *Sizzling Thumb?*

Eliot knocked gently on the door of the suite. I had never seen him so nervous. He'd invited me to go with him to the Pierre Hotel to interview Weber Gregston, whose new film *Sorrow and Son* had everyone talking. I'd seen it and liked it very much, but people really paid to see what this Gregston character was going to do next.

He was a strange man who had made only three films in ten years and paid little attention to what either Hollywood or the public wanted. A decade before, he had been an obscure young poet who had abruptly come into the public eye when he *1.* won a MacArthur Fellowship and then *2.* used most of the money to make a low-budget black and white film about a man who was convinced he was his own wife. It won a special award at the Berlin Film Festival and purportedly caused a riot in St. Louis, Missouri. One of the things I liked about the movie was its title—*The Night is Blond.*

But the thing I liked most about his movies was the photography. Weber Gregston saw things in ways that either rang bells in your subconscious (hey, I never thought of it *that* way before . . . !) or else amazed you with new angles and colour combinations and visions of life that were not only unique and compelling, but also utterly recognizable and understandable at the same time.

While we waited, Eliot shifted his briefcase from hand to hand and made faces at me. Gregston rarely gave interviews and had allowed this one only because he thought what Eliot Kilbertus had said about his last picture, *How to Put on Your Hat,* was 'offensive and interesting'.

When he finally opened the door, neither Eliot nor I knew what to do, so we just stood there and waited for Gregston's first move. But he didn't move; he stood there and looked at us coolly. The first words that came to my mind were 'Scotland' or 'Wales'. If his ancestors hadn't come from that part of the world, I would have been very surprised. He was a handsome man in his late thirties, but handsome in a rugged, burly way; he looked like a rugby player or an athlete who liked to jump in the mud and mix it up with the boys. His deep-set green eyes were quiet and reserved, his red-brown hair could have used a good brushing. He was wearing a teeshirt that said 'AIDA COFFEE AND TEA RESEARCH VIENNA, AUSTRIA' and a pair of leather pants, the colour of a candy bar, which must have cost as much as a Mercedes-Benz. He had on white gym-socks and no shoes.

'You're Kilbertus?'

'Yes. Hello.' Eliot put out his hand to shake, but Gregston ignored it and looked at me.

'Who's your friend?' He gave me an amazingly cold once-over. Well, I thought to myself, Fuck *you*, Weber.

'This is my friend, Cullen James. If you object to her being here, then I'm not interested in interviewing you.'

'Wowie Zowie!' Gregston smiled sunnily and whipped one of his hands down in a pretend-karate chop. 'Tough guys! Come in, *both* of you. Cullen, huh? What kind of name is that?'

He didn't wait for an answer. As he turned back into the room, Eliot gave him the finger and blew me a silent kiss. We followed him into a living-room where the remnants of someone's breakfast lay unattractively on a side table.

While Eliot set up his tape recorder, Gregston flopped down on a couch and looked me over again. 'You didn't answer my question. Where does "Cullen" come from?'

I shrugged and wanted to go home. He had already popped my hero-worship balloon and I wasn't about to let him get to any others. I felt like a drowning person who's going down for the last time —only it was Gregston's life that raced through my mind rather than my own. Here was a prime example of a nasty, lucky son of a bitch who had probably got every woman he'd ever wanted by spitting in her eye. How many sad, sappy women had let him do that, then felt 'privileged' to say they had spent a night or two under Weber Gregston . . . in every way?

69

Yet once the interview began, he opened up and showed both a brilliance and an insight which made it clear where all of those good movies had come from. Most of the time he spoke in a quiet, indifferent voice; later, Eliot said it was the kind you hear giving the stock prices over the radio. In the same tone he would talk about an old lover of his who had recently committed suicide, or a dwarf-throwing contest in Australia. I didn't know if he was putting on an act, but judging from both his initial rudeness and this distant tone of voice, I got the feeling he didn't give much of a damn what we thought of him.

About half-way through, Eliot excused himself to go to the bathroom. As soon as he was gone, Gregston asked if I would like to spend the rest of the day with him.

'No, thanks.'

'How come?'

'Well, partly because I don't like you, but mostly because I do like my husband and daughter.'

'Sticking to your guns, huh?' I think he was taken aback, but there was a faint stench of mockery in his voice. He rubbed his knees and nodded to himself. 'Now you can go home and tell your husband you said "No". He'll like that.'

'Look—' I was about to say something, but decided to leave instead. As I got up, I asked him to tell Eliot I'd gone home and would meet him there.

'Maybe I should ask *Eliot* to blow me, so it won't be a total waste.'

'He wouldn't be able to *find* it, Weber.'

My back was turned when I said that, so I didn't see him get up. But faster than hell, I felt his hand on my shoulder, wrenching me around to face him. No man had ever touched me like that. Up close, he looked ten feet tall and as mean as a snake. Terrified, I flung up my arms to protect my face.

He drew back his hand to slap me, I think. I stuck one of mine out to block him and even at that ferocious moment, I thought how ridiculous it must have looked—like a cop directing traffic.

A giant arc of purple light flared out from the middle of my palm. I knew that light—I'd seen it in the dreams: Rondua light, Bones of the Moon light.

'Stay away!'

70

The light struck Gregston square in the chest and knocked him back across the room.

My hand, the light now gone, stayed extended towards him.

The babysitter had left and I was on the couch with Mae held tight to my chest when the doorbell rang. I got up and let in a wildly-grinning Eliot.

'Cullen James, what did you *do?* I went out of that room for five minutes! When I got back, you were gone, Gregston was on his ass and he was looking at the door like Hitler had just left. What *happened?*'

'Nothing. He's a hateful, horrible, *horrible* man.'

'*That's* why you left? Why, I'm horrible and you like *me.*'

'Eliot, please just shut up. Could you leave me alone now?'

Mae patted my cheeks and it was hard for me to keep from crying.

'Cullen—'

'Just *go,* Eliot! Okay? I'll call you later.'

'Stop it! Calm down. Do you want some tea?'

He looked at me worriedly and walked into the kitchen. Half of me hated him for staying, the other half was grateful for his company. Being alone at that moment would have been bad.

The scene in the hotel room kept replaying in my mind in slow motion. My raised hand and open fingers, the blast of wavy purple light, Gregston catching it in the chest and flying away. It reminded me of watching Lopez's car crash on television: replay after slow replay until you couldn't help memorizing the worst. But this time it was my own mind that kept re-running the film and not some hot-shot television producer in a control room. Raised hand, open fingers, shot of light . . .

'Eliot!'

He ran into the room with a cup and saucer in his hands.

'Eliot, please sit down and let me tell you this. Don't say *anything* until I've told you every little bit.'

I told him everything. And when I was alone, what made me love him very much was that he didn't ask me one sceptical question. He believed me, thank God.

'Okay, Cullen. Let me call Mary. She'll tell us what's up, one way or the other.'

'Who's Mary?' The last thing I wanted was another person, a

stranger, in my living-room. It felt like my whole life was in the middle of the worst earthquake in ages.

'Mary's a good friend of mine who's probably the best palmist in New York. If anyone can tell what's happening to you now, it's her. You have to trust me on this one, Cullen. All I can say is that if the same thing had happened to me, I'd call Mary first and wait to hear what she had to say after she looked at my hand.'

'Oh shit, I hate this. I can't tell you how much I hate this whole damned thing.'

An hour later the doorbell rang and Eliot went to answer it. I wasn't any calmer, but being at home and having a friend there who knew the whole strange truth made it more bearable.

Eliot came back in, followed by a good-looking thirty-ish woman with short hair, large soft eyes and a confident smile. I liked her looks.

'Cullen James, this is Mary Miller. Mary, we want you to do a complete reading. The total works, okay?'

'Sure, Eliot. Hi, Cullen! Have you ever done this before? No? It's real easy and you don't have to be scared or anything.'

She sat down next to me and, to my surprise, took out the kind of rubber roller you use to make linoleum blockprints, a tube of black ink and some sheets of white paper.

Opening the tube, she took my hands and squeezed a sizeable blob onto both palms. Eliot hadn't told me about this part, so I looked up at him to see what was going on.

'Some palmists do it this way, Cullen. They don't even look at your hand—just the print on the paper when it's done.'

Mary rolled the jet-black ink evenly over and over my palms, then turned them down on to the paper for a print. She was dissatisfied with the first two, so we did the whole thing again. I felt as if I had been arrested and was being booked and finger-printed.

'Okay, Cullen. I've got it now. These last two will be fine. You can go and wash your hands; that ink comes right off. While you're in there, I'll have a good look at these prints. Take your time.'

I left for the bathroom, followed closely by Eliot. While I scrubbed away in the basin with soap and a pumice stone, he reminded me not to say a word to Mary once she got started. To let her do all the talking and not give her any hints about myself or what had just happened. Outside information could confuse or distract her and that would badly affect things.

When we walked back into the room I was scared, but the expression on her face was okay. She was looking at Eliot.

'I don't know what happened, Eliot, but from everything I can see here, she's absolutely fine.' She looked down at the pieces of paper in front of her and nodded.

'Cullen, I can give you a life reading or a crisis reading. But it sounds like you want a crisis reading?'

'Yes, I guess I do.' I looked at Eliot, who nodded and put his finger to his lips.

'Okay, then I'd say you have nothing to worry about. In fact, I'm very surprised you're having any kind of trouble. Everything in your hand says you're all right. Your marriage is balanced, but you already know that. Sometimes you wish your husband was a little bit more exciting and zippy, but besides that . . . Your children have inherited that healthy balance. They also trust you, which is extremely important.'

'You mean my *child*. I have only one.'

Eliot shushed me and wiggled his finger for me to be quiet.

'If you believe in reincarnation, it says you've lived several very interesting lives and have learned from them. What's most important in a reading like this, a crisis reading, is that there's no death in your hand now, Cullen.' She looked at me and smiled reassuringly. 'Your father was very ill recently, wasn't he? Anyway, you're still worried that he'll die soon, but he won't. He has a few years to go yet and having you around has made both him and your mother tremendously happy. They're both in seventh heaven about having a grandchild; it makes them feel stronger and necessary again. Your husband had some kind of trouble a few months ago—Something to do with his body, but also his work. Anyway, he's completely recovered and likes the path his life has taken. And by the way, he loves you very much. That's all over your hand.' She pointed to a few lines here and there and I looked at them as if I knew what she was talking about. 'When I do a crisis reading, people are usually worried either about death or some kind of disaster. Neither thing is *anywhere* on your hand now.

'Just the opposite, actually! It's sort of difficult to describe this, but it's as if your life is at peace now. I've seen this kind of pattern before in people who are terminally ill, but who have overcome their fear of death. Don't get me wrong though—there's not a sign of death in or near you now, but you seem to have resolved some-

73

thing that is very hard for most of us to resolve. Like accepting our own deaths, or something else like that.

'When you were younger, you tore yourself apart with contradictions, like so many of us do. You were distant from everyone, but then you turned round and gave yourself to a man who ate you alive. It was a big disaster, right? It was like the Push Me-Pull You in *Doctor Dolittle*, remember? One half went one way, the other the other? Well, that was you then. But you're not that way now. Your feet are on the ground because subconsciously you know you're both needed and loved by a number of people, and those are the two things everyone wants most out of life. You want to be loved and you want to know there are a bunch of people who need you, specifically *you*. If you had asked for a life reading, I'd have told you you're a very lucky woman. You *are* a very lucky woman! There's a great deal of love both in and towards you, if you get what I mean. I haven't seen so much in a person's palm for a long time. It radiates right out of there in all kinds of directions. It's your base, it's like your main ingredient. There is *no* crisis here, Cullen. I can guarantee that, and I don't usually say things like that unless I'm absolutely sure.'

I knew Eliot would disapprove of my prompting, but I had to ask. 'What about my dreams? I've been having a series of *really* strange dreams. Sometimes they're so strong and vivid that they scare me.'

'There are signs of a very strong fantasy life in your hand, that's for sure. Your imagination is vivid and it probably carries over into your night dreams. Is that what you mean?'

'Well, not really. What if I said I think I have "powers", or something?' I felt so much like a goony ass saying that that I couldn't even look at Mary to see what her expression was.

'You don't have to be embarrassed, Cullen, there really *are* people who have them. But if you do, they don't show up in your hand. Sometimes special powers arise from a situation; we don't have them in us innately. You know what I mean—a child is run over by a car and the mother is able to pick up the car by the front bumper to save the kid. Or we're threatened physically and suddenly have tremendous strength to defend ourselves: a kind of strength that goes away immediately after the danger passes. Even scientists admit to that kind of phenomena, although they attribute it to things like adrenalin rushes. Who knows for sure about these things?

'All I can tell you, Cullen, is that your hand shows no powers. So I don't think they're *your* powers if they do exist. In your palm it shows you're protected by others, but not by powers. Whoever it is, *they* won't let anything happen to you, if it is at all possible.'

She took my hand and looked at it closely for a long minute. 'No, I don't see any powers here. A giant amount of love, but no powers.'

How strange it was to eat glass and light. All of the food on the table was laid out beautifully and precisely. The spread would have looked delicious if everything hadn't been transparent; splashing the light from the icy chandelier hung high and huge over the crystalline dining-table.

Pepsi picked up his clear hot-dog wrapped in its clear bun and took a big bite. His walking stick leaned against the chair and was the only patch of colour around. Exposed to the sun for days on our walk here, the sticks had burned or ripened . . . changed from their original grey-brown to a deep, vivid purple.

Sizzling Thumb had mine over his lap and kept petting it like a cat. 'Your tapes arrived without chickens.'

When we'd reached his castle earlier that morning, he had greeted us at the drawbridge by saying 'Doughnuts and staples, remember!'

Luckily Mr Tracy had prepared us and was there to translate. 'He's welcoming us. Says his home is ours as long as we want it. Give him your walking stick, Cullen.'

I did and the man's bright old face lit up. 'Scare butt plum jabs!'

Sizzling Thumb was the first human we had seen on Rondua and despite the jumble of words, his presence was tremendously reassuring. He wore a suit made entirely of newspapers, as did everyone in the castle. On closer inspection, I saw that the newspaper was the one Eliot wrote for, *Tic-Toc*.

This jolly old fellow controlled the entire Fourth Stroke of Rondua—the southern section we had been crossing ever since our arrival—and his castle sat on the border with the north. I was required to turn the first Bone over to him if we were to pass on unharmed. There had been no mention of Pepsi surrendering his.

The King of the Fourth Stroke worshipped light, so everything around him was there to serve and complement it; not argue or distort. We were treated well, but with the distance and respect usually afforded ambassadors from remote, questionable countries. Everyone stared uncomprehendingly at us in our multi-coloured clothes and sneakers. No one paid any attention to the animals.

We were given a tour of the castle and shown little cars that ran on solar power, rooms where reflections were stored, museums that housed perfect diamonds and glass noodles. Everything was certainly solid and real, but I kept feeling I was either stoned or under water the whole time. Later on, at the end of the tour, I hesitantly asked why everyone wore newspaper suits. Sizzling Thumb smiled and put out his hand and one of the butlers put a magnifying glass in it. The king walked over to a window and, holding the glass this way and that, focused sunlight on to a small piece of his suit in the middle of his stomach. In a few seconds the suit started to smoke, then caught fire underneath the glass with a slight 'puff' sound. Alarmed, I looked at him to make sure he knew what he was doing.

'Hot light!' He watched the flame catch hold of everything and burn right up. The suit was one big orange blaze in a few seconds, but none of the servants did a thing. Pieces of ash like black snowflakes floated wispily up and down and everywhere around us. Sizzling Thumb flapped his arms up and down like a fat bird on fire. The air was full of ash and pieces of flaming newspaper.

Minutes later, he stood there naked and untouched and jaunty as ever.

After the banquet was over and everyone had toasted everyone else, Sizzling Thumb (in a brand-new suit) banged his goblet down for quiet.

'The hat looks like it wants to say something.'

I smiled and nodded and waited for the Mr Tracy translation.

'Sizzling Thumb says the north has very bad weather now. That will make it very difficult for us to find the second Bone. He says he doesn't even think Pepsi's walking-stick will help us, but I don't believe that.'

'What's he going to do with mine, Mr Tracy?' I looked at it on the old man's lap, not without a lot of sadness; I had grown very used to having it in the dome of my hand.

'It's his protection, Cullen. The entire Fourth Stroke is safe now.'

'And what about us? Are we safe too?'

'Yes, as long as Pepsi keeps his.'

'But isn't he too young? He doesn't understand everything yet.'

Mr Tracy turned and nodded to Pepsi, who was sitting on his other side. 'Tell your mother the Law of Stolen Flight.'

'Only flame, and things with wings. All the rest suffer stings.'

'Mr Tracy? Where did that come from?'

'From no one, Cullen. You should remember all this. Pepsi's change has begun. He *will* find the second Bone because he owns the important half of the first. You found it for him. After he owns the second, then he will be stronger than all of us.'

The North was dark with clouds and impending war. As soon as we crossed the border, we met up with dragoons of Heeg, the lizard King. These soldiers rode giant iguanas the colour of stone and grass and were dressed in garish uniforms that reminded me of Hapsburg outfits Danny and I had seen in a military museum in Italy.

Once we had shown them Pepsi's walking stick, they treated us with brusque respect. Nevertheless, they warned us to travel only in the day because their patrols might otherwise mistake us for the enemy who had been steadily moving in from the West for the past few weeks.

A day later we met this 'enemy'. They looked exactly like Heeg's men, only this bunch was all in grey: uniforms, sabres, iguanas. But they were awed by Pepsi's stick and asked if there was anything they could do for us. They treated us to a delicious meal of grey food.

Later we watched them ride off and wondered which of them would survive their coming battles.

The wolf rubbed her nose with a paw. The camel quietly chewed his cud. The dog looked at me.

'It wasn't like this before, was it, Mr Tracy? We used to come to the North to watch the thunderstorms and wash our clothes in the rain.'

Felina spoke. 'It's never been like this before. I have cousins by the sea who march in file and sharpen their teeth on wet coral. There's greed and treachery everywhere. It used to make us sad, but now we're frightened. Aren't we?' She looked at the dog and the camel and they nodded.

'Are we going to fight too?' Pepsi waved his stick around in the air like a sword.

'You're going to *stop* the fighting, Pepsi. You and your mother.'

Martio stretched his long camel's neck and gazed down the railway track into the silent, empty distance. It had rained again and the steel rails shone a wet, silvery blue.

'Don't sit down, Pepsi. You'll get your pants wet.'

'I'm tired, Mommy! I want to go to sleep!'

He hardly ever whined or complained, so the day's trip across the North to this railway line must have been harder on him than we'd thought. We'd been moving since dawn. Sizzling Thumb had said it was imperative we walk and not ride the animals at all across the Third Stroke. However, that cut our pace to about a tenth of what it had been before.

The train was due at any time. There was no station where we were, only a place where the road crossed the narrow, meandering railway track. The train would take us to Kempinski, the capital city of Rondua where the first of Pepsi's great tests would take place.

The brown sky and fall of late afternoon light left us all quiet and still. There was nothing to do but wait and think about what we had seen and heard that day.

Purple Jakes lived in the North. Purple Jakes and Yellow-striped Drews that ate cheese pies and slept furious or in fear of everything. Every one of them, bright neon things moving fast against the dark-earth colours of that landscape. Besides the colours, if you asked me to try and describe them, I would smile.

Do you know the pictures children draw when they're first given crayons and paper? Those wild red slashes, or thick blobby blue circles that spill and shoot off the page and have nothing to do with one another? Those were the Jakes and Drews, the major inhabitants of this stroke of Rondua. Heeg ruled this section, but it was a mystery to me what he and his men controlled besides a certain piece of hilly land on a map. Beside his grey soldiers and their lizards, there were no 'living' beings here that had any kind of recognizable form.

Something else too: I have no idea what language they spoke or even how they communicated, because every time we saw one of them that strange day, they were far off in the distance moving in the opposite direction.

Felina said no one she knew had ever seen a Jake or a Drew close-up. Like shy rare birds, the scribbled-looking things fled from everyone. The only way you could recognize them was by their brilliantly distinctive colours.

'If they're always running away, why does Heeg have to have an Army? Who's here to conquer? Who's his enemy?'

78

'The *land*, Cullen. Heeg wants to own the Stroke. But if the land doesn't like the leader, it rebels.'

'Rebels? How?'

'Look up at the sky. Look at the land here. Everything is either wet and soggy, or too bright and quivering, like the Jakes.'

'But Felina, I remember it used to rain here before. We had fun then.'

'You were too young, Cullen, to see what was really going on. It was beginning even back then. But we knew you were leaving, so we didn't want to worry you by telling you the truth. We knew that you'd come back some day. All that you've seen so far is what happened after you left Rondua to go back to the other side.'

Far off in the distance, a train whistle *queeched* once.

'Well, are there a lot of people like Heeg around in Rondua?'

'There aren't any shadows on a cloudy day, Cullen. None at all before a storm, because *everything* is darker then. Our weather here has been cloudy for years. The Third Stroke is only one example.'

The train whistle slashed through the air again, much closer this time. Pepsi, Martio and Felina moved towards the sound. Mr Tracy and I stayed where we were.

'When you were first here, Cullen, we had hoped you would be the heir who could save us from all this. But you weren't, although you came very close. We let you go when you were a child, because children are wonderfully selfish and remember only what matters to them at the time. And those are always small things—the colour of the cake at their birthday party, or who gave them a Valentine at the second-grade party last Wednesday. But adults remember so much more, whether they like it or not. When you were a child we wanted you to go away clear and empty and happy, so you would have only good memories of your time in Rondua. Then one day you would voluntarily bring us an heir who *would* have the power to make it right here again.'

His last words disappeared in the clamour of the arriving train which passed in a slowing rush of clanks and spits and hot oiled metal.

I yelled to him over the noise, '*Is* Pepsi the one? Does he have what you need?'

'Yes! We think so! If we're lucky!'

'But what if you're wrong? What if he's not the one?'

'We all die.'

Kempinski would have been miraculous if we hadn't been in Rondua so long and hadn't seen so much already. Giant animals like our three friends strolled the streets. People dressed in bizarre clothes and living hats moved by in a hurried crush. Different kinds of outlandish music accompanied us everywhere; much of it was reedy, mysterious and oriental. It was a suitable background for belly-dancers and fire-eaters, or walking through a bazaar in Baghdad or Jerusalem.

At one point I started laughing when we passed a movie theatre that said it was showing 'WEBER GREGSTON'S NEWEST MASTERPIECE—SORROW AND SON'.

Pepsi held my hand and asked two hundred questions about what we were doing and what we were seeing. I answered as best I could, but my knowledge and memories of Kempinski were dim or clouded by the years I had been away. I had little spots of memory—I knew that that street led to the 'Avenue of Napping Bull Terriers' and that we had to buy some coily from a street vendor because it was the best chewing-gum around, but little else.

We arrived early in the morning and spent most of the day tramping through the city seeing the sights, trying to remember what it had been like when I'd been there before. We fed the Weez and Daybuck at the Zoo of Blind Animals, ate a big lunch of marucks and toocha juice out in the ricefields at the edge of town.

As a lavender and grey dusk set in, we made our way to the amphitheatre at the centre of the city. Every time we turned a corner that day, the building had loomed up in front of us, colossal and old beyond belief but perfectly preserved. Now people streamed into its many entrances unhindered by any ticket-takers.

The night before, Mr Tracy had said going to the theatre was the only necessary thing we had to do while we were in Kempinski. What happened there would determine how long we would have to remain in the capital. He made no mention of why, or what was supposed to go on in that ancient place.

The murmur of the crowd died down quickly when a man appeared on the small stage in the centre of the theatre, just as we were sitting down on one of the stone benches. His clothing was nondescript and his voice was high and thin, unimpressive.

'Today is the third day of the Search. If contestants fail to build the Wind's Lips again today, the next round will be held as usual in two months' time.'

The people sitting around us didn't react. Eager for things to begin, they were apparently well aware of what the announcer was saying.

'May we have the shapes, please?'

For the next ten minutes, men dressed like different kinds of vegetables brought out transparent glass-like blocks which looked like the blocks children play with. These were much larger, however; larger and lighter, because the men carried them on six or seven at a time.

When they were done, about forty-five or fifty of the things sat in a sloppy heap off to one side of the stage. They came in all sizes; some looked like the boxes you carry long-stemmed roses in, others were larger than a phone booth.

'What are they for, Mom?'

The memory loomed into view like a slowly rising fish. I remembered. What do we know? How much have we forgotten? Is Ronduan history swimming away in all of our minds, only way down deep where the murky things live?

Pepsi pulled on my sleeve. *'Mom,* what are they for?'

'One day a child was playing with blocks exactly like those, Pepsi. By accident, they put them together so specially that they made something called "The Wind's Lips". Somehow, whenever the wind blew through it, it was able to whistle perfect songs.'

'The wind or the lips, Mom?'

'Well, we need our lips to blow, don't we, Peps?'

'What happened to these lips? Did they die?'

'Somebody knocked them down a long time ago. But they've been trying to put them back together that same way ever since. No one's been able to do it.'

'What happens if they do make it again, Mom? Do the songs come back?'

Nearby, a man with three hands was listening to us and smiling. Leaning over, he said what I expected to hear: 'If you're the one to do it, Sonny, you'll win one of the Bones of the Moon.'

I looked at him. 'And only children are allowed to try, aren't they?'

'Naturally! A child did it first, so only a child will have the ability to do it again. Go ahead up to the table, boy. Give us back our music

81

and win your mother the Bone!' He looked at us, then laughed and laughed as if we were the funniest things he had seen all day.

After the first gasps, silence fell on the amphitheatre like a sword. Pepsi stood back and listened, with the rest of us, to the growing swirl of music pouring from the form he had made with the blocks. The shape he had come up with in the end looked vaguely like one of those space needle/restaurant things, but it had certainly done the trick. Every sound imaginable poured out of there: Iraqi grunting music, *a capella* French children's songs, bird whistles, disco tunes. At one point, I heard a few bars of Danny's favourite Frank Sinatra song. A United Nations of music. Pepsi delighted everyone by turning round and shrugging helplessly at us; as if to say that he didn't understand it either, folks.

The Grand Mayor of Kempinski, Larcquo Hednut, came on stage and presented Pepsi with the prize: a greenish-gold Bone of the Moon that was shaped like a whistling face.

People and animals cheered and applauded. But the most interesting thing to me was that when the presentation ceremony was over, the majority of them filed out of the theatre exactly as they'd come in: no hosannas were sung, the victor wasn't carried out on people's shoulders . . . Old women scolded their grandchildren for dawdling, and two yellow lions tried to decide on where to eat dinner.

I waited a while and then walked down to the stage. Hednut had his arm on Pepsi's shoulder and from the serious look on the mayor's face, was in the middle of talking man-to-man.

'Pepsi?'

'Hi, Mom. Hednut says he knows Martio.'

The other turned to me and bowed deeply. 'Weasel tippler, thread clock.'

We were back to Sizzling Thumb-talk. Where was Mr Tracy?

To my surprise, Pepsi let out his silliest laugh. When he'd calmed down a little, he spluttered out, 'Did you understand that, Mom? Hednut says the last time he saw *you*, you always lost your shoes!'

As Hednut rattled on and Pepsi followed, I realized too well that he understood this crazy talk word for word now. I clenched both fists very tightly and was scared. The second Bone, or Pepsi's growing powers, or something equally strong was quickly taking him far away from me towards . . . what?

82

*

'Mr Tracy, I don't understand *anything.*'

Our friends had been waiting for us outside the amphitheatre. All three congratulated Pepsi and admired the Bone, but for the most part they were very cool about his recent accomplishment.

'If building these "Wind's Lips" is supposed to be such a big thing, how come everyone in there was so ho-hum about it after he did it?'

'Because it's been done so many times before, Cullen. You did it too when you were young.'

'I did? *I* built those Lips?'

'You did.'

'And I won the Bone? The exact same one?'

'Yes.'

I sucked the inside of one cheek before going on, 'What happened after that? After I got it?'

'There are five Bones, Cullen. Do you remember their names yet?'

'Yes, all of the names came to me today when we were walking around town. Obnoy, Kat, Domenica, Slee and Min.'

'That's right. Together they represent the Four Strokes of Rondua and the capital, Kempinski.

'If someone wants to rule Rondua, they must possess all five of the Bones. What's wonderful about the rule is that to acquire each one, a person must possess a certain good quality. For example, to find the first, Obnoy, one must be loved; must be lov*able.* Taken together, these qualities are what would make someone a great ruler.'

'Obnoy was the one I gave to Sizzling Thumb?'

'You gave him your *half.* Only Pepsi's was important. The one he achieved this afternoon, Kat, could only be got with imagination and inventiveness. Rebuilding "The Wind's Lips" for Kempinski proved he had those qualities.'

'But you said even I built them once.' I watched Pepsi walking in front of me, his small white hand resting on the camel's large brown flank.

'Yes, when you were a girl we were all very excited because you grabbed up the first four Bones so quickly. We were sure you would be the next ruler. We had great hopes.'

'But then I flopped, eh?'

'Then you flopped.'

'Why? What did I do wrong?'

'For the Fifth Bone, Min, you needed very great courage, and you didn't have it.'

'Uh oh.'

We walked on in a gloomy silence, my eyes hard on my little son's small back. I had a bad, dry taste inside my mouth. 'Is he going to be in a lot of danger, Mr Tracy?'

The dog smiled cheerlessly and dipped his head yes.

6

Weber Gregston called me.

'What do *you* want? How did you get my number?'

'From the phone book. I called all the Jameses. Look, I've got to talk to you. I'm sorry for what happened.'

'Fine, you're sorry. Now go away. Leave me alone.'

'I can't, it's too important. Please don't hang up, Cullen. Look, I *have* to see you.'

His voice was human and fragile. It was as if we were both fifteen and he was asking me out for a first date. I was positive his hands were shaking.

'Weber, tell me something, okay? Are your hands shaking? Tell the truth.'

He laughed. 'Yes. How did you know? I took my gloves off a minute ago because they were so hot.'

'Telepathy. What do you want to talk about?'

'I want to apologize. I want to tell you . . . Look, I have to see you. You have to say yes, just give me a few minutes.'

'I don't know. Your reasons are lousy. I accept your apology, but what else is there to talk about? You were rude, you're apologizing, so now it's over. *Basta finito.'*

'Cullen, I've been standing in this . . . in this phone booth for half an hour, sweating bullets and dialling wrong numbers. You don't know how damned hard it was for me to get up the nerve to get in touch with you. I'm telling you the truth.'

I didn't change one piece of clothing (although I was tempted to) or put on any make-up. I took Mae along in her stroller for added insurance. The first time I had met Weber Gregston, I had tried to look like a dream. Now I looked like the 'Before' part of a dandruff commercial.

I met him a few blocks from the house. He stood on a corner with his hands in the pockets of a Gianni Versace leather jacket I had seen advertised that month in *Vogue*. It was beyond beautiful, and the kind of thing you'd think a famous movie director *would* wear. I liked seeing his big bulk in it; it softened some of the hard edges of his tough-guy face.

'Oh, am I glad you came! Is that your baby?' He looked pleased.

'That's my baby.'

'Hello, baby. What's his name?'

'Mae.'

'Hiya, Mae. Funny name for a boy.'

Despite an earlier resolve to be cold and sceptical with him, I burst out laughing. I love people who say funny, crooked things. Weber looked at me, genuinely surprised I had laughed at his joke.

'What do you want, Weber? Don't pull down like that on your pockets. You'll stretch the leather.'

'I feel nine years old, Cullen. I've been thinking about you for a week. I was supposed to be in Florida today, but I stayed here because of you. Honest to God! Because of you!'

'Don't sound so astonished—you'll ruin the compliment! I don't understand, Weber. The last time I saw you, you were nasty and fresh. Today you want to go steady with me. I think you'd better go to Florida.' I checked Mae to see if she was still properly tucked in.

'No, it's not that simple. There's more to it. Can we go somewhere and talk?'

'Nope, but I have some shopping to do and you can come along if you like.'

'Okay, I guess that'll have to do. Are you sure you don't want to have a sandwich? We can take Mae and get him a hamburger.'

I was enjoying my little, momentary power over him and wasn't about to give it up for a sandwich. 'No. You either go with us to the market or *niente.*'

Once inside the market, he slipped on a pair of battered horn-rimmed glasses which made him look very different—sort of like a red-headed Clark Kent.

He caught me sizing him up in them.

'You know where I got these glasses? Aren't they ugly? They belonged to my grandfather, Zolie Dale. Everyone in the family called him Zolie Dale the Illiterate though, because he couldn't read. Isn't that a terrible handle to give someone?'

'How did you get the glasses?'

'That's the interesting part of the story. The last time I ever saw him, he was sick in bed with stomach cancer, he told me to take the glasses when he died and have them changed to my prescription. "That way, boy, they'll be able to spend part of their life reading up on all the things they missed." '

Weber switched into a perfect Southern accent when he pretended to be his grandfather.

We left the stroller in the doorway and he slid Mae into the baby seat of the metal cart. It felt strange doing these small, familiar, intimate things with someone so famous. For a while I dreamed I was in a movie with him; somewhere off in the distance was a camera and a whole slew of people watching us shoot the scene. 'Take One—Cullen and Weber in the supermarket. Roll 'em!'

He tickled Mae under the chin. She was wholly unimpressed and looked at him stonily.

He pushed the cart while I walked alongside, checking my shopping list and stealing glances at him whenever I thought he wouldn't see me. We'd picked up milk and baby food before he started talking.

'I had to find you, Cullen. Have you ever had that feeling about a person? They make you crazy? Who *are* you?'

'Helen of Troy. Weber, what are you talking about?'

'I'm talking about being fucking *haunted* by you. I don't usually get hit by women, and I never get hit and then want to see them again, that's for sure.'

'Weber, I'm married. I have the beautiful Mae, as you can see with your own eyes, and I just ain't interested. Besides, you're famous and have the reputation for being very mysterious. What woman wouldn't be fascinated by that? That's the most romantic combination there is.'

'*You* don't want it. I can't be too romantic if you're giving me the brush-off in a supermarket.' He looked around. 'In between the nacho chips and the onion dip. Hey, I forgot to ask, where did you learn karate? You know, when you bopped me like that? My chest hurt for an hour afterwards.'

'Hey, man, you're Weber Gregston, right?' A punk with fingernail clippers for earrings grabbed Weber by the arm. I was intrigued to see how he would handle it. On second thoughts, I got scared when the thought crossed my mind that Weber might just punch the kid on the chin.

I was wrong. He stuck out his hand to shake. 'Yes, I am. Hi! How are you?'

'Fuck you, man. I think your new movie's the shits. Ha! I bet none of those asshole critics ever told you *that!*'

Weber's face was impossible to read and I realized my body had tensed up.

'Well, okay, you hate them. I'm sorry about that. We'll be seeing you.'

'And this is your little wife? Shit, Bigshot Weber Gregston in a market! Where are the Cocoa-Pops, Mr Director? You gonna do a close-up of her by the TV dinners?'

I assumed Weber was going to heave him into the frozen foods. Instead, he started making crazy faces at the boy. His mouth went up and down and his tongue came out. Then he rubbed his forehead back and forth and turned it bright red. It was something to see.

The punk didn't know what to do. He'd expected some kind of 'Gunfight at the Market' but instead got Weber Gregston going crazy on him.

To make things worse (and funnier), Weber started bumping him with his chest and saying the names of cities, still making those faces the whole time.

'Detroit! Louisville!' Bump.

'What's your problem, Gregston?'

'Phoenix. Boise.' Bump. Bump.

The punk looked at me, angry and defenceless.

'What's with him?'

'Houston!' Bump. 'Shreveport!' Bump.

'You fuckin' nut! You can't direct and now you're nuts!' He stepped back and hit a potato chip display; then he picked up a bag as if he was going to throw it but decided to disappear instead.

'Creep! Wacko!' He walked fast down the aisle, checking us over his shoulder all the while.

When he was gone, Weber shook his head and looked down at Mae. His performance had caught her fancy and he had her full attention. He smiled and wriggled his tongue at her and she cooed.

'Where was I?'

'Does that happen to you a lot?'

'Right after a film comes out sometimes. They put my picture in the paper . . .' He shrugged. 'Cullen, what am I going to do about you? Huh?'

I stopped and looked at him square-on. 'If I'm so enticing, how come you were so mean to me the other day?'

'Because I'm a pig and sometimes people scare me. I wanted you and thought you were different from the way you are. It's part of the stupid game. Who knows? Cullen, look, I don't remember people's faces. But ever since we met, all I've done is walk around with yours in my head. How long were we together, half an hour? And you want to hear the weirdest part? As soon as you knocked me down, that's when I started wanting you. When you first came in the room I just thought, here's a good-looking woman; let's see if she's interested. But after you *hit* me, I couldn't get you out of my mind. That's the absolute truth!'

We walked on in silence and I found the rest of my groceries. At the check-out counter, he tried to pay for them but I wouldn't let him.

When we were outside, we stood for too long looking carefully at each other. That's Weber Gregston, famous movie director, Cullen. And he wants you. What do you think of *that?*

'Did you really call up all the Jameses in the phone book?'

'Every one—you were the seventeenth. Check it out in the book. It took me three days to get the courage to even pick up the phone.'

Another silence and then I reached over and straightened his collar.

'I'm completely honoured, Weber, but we can't. I like who I'm with and I like who I am. Finally. You know what I mean?' He smiled and nodded and looked at his shoe. 'It took too long to get here and I don't want to chance throwing it away. There's a big part of me that would *love* to have an affair with you, but I'm just not going to do it.'

'There's not even a chance? We could go to the movies or something.'

He didn't even know what he was saying any more, and that touched me more deeply than anything he had said so far. The irony of his last sentence almost went by unnoticed as a result. Then he grinned and touched my arm. 'I hear the new Weber Gregston film is a real piece of shit. You heard what the guy in there said. You wanna go?'

The moment had passed and we were on comfortably safe ground again.

'Naah, I already saw it eleven times.' I looked at his chest. 'That's a beautiful jacket, you know. Don't ruin it by sticking your hands in the pockets like that.' I looked at him and he smiled for a second, then let it fall away. 'Weber, there's no chance. I am glad you came shopping with us. Mae too; she hasn't giggled like that in a week. You make funnier faces than I do.'

He kissed his fingertips and touched them to my forehead. 'I'll see you. Jesus, I'd better stop thinking about you.'

I watched him walk away, then I took a deep breath and rolled my eyes. Queen for a Day.

'Package for James.'

I undid all of the locks and opened the door for the United Parcel Service man. The box was brown and large and for me. No return address and no sign of what store it came from. A surprise from Danny or my parents?

When I pulled the tissue paper aside and saw what it was, I groaned and sat back on my haunches. A Gianni Versace leather jacket exactly like Weber's. The stuff that dreams are made of. Brand-new and smelling—even there in the box—as heavenly as only a new piece of beautiful clothing can smell.

'Oh, Weber. Oh boy!'

The middle of the afternoon and it was snowing again. I wondered if he was somewhere in the city in this snow, or else under a Florida orange tree very far away.

The jacket was a size too large, but I liked that. It reminded me of wearing my boy-friend's letter sweater back in high school. I walked around the room for some time with my hands in my new pockets, feeling pretty damned special and glamorous. I showed Mae, but she was more interested in her mobile. All this was followed by a long posing session in front of the bathroom mirror.

I discovered the envelope in the inside front pocket. Knowing who it was from and wondering what it would say, I opened it but then only held it in my hand before daring to take out the letter and read what was written there.

'First there's Pepsi and Mr Tracy and now Weber Gregston. My God!'

The handwriting was unexpectedly small and 'straight-A student' careful. I smiled and touched my lips when I saw it was a poem.

NIGHT MEDALLION by Daniel Mark Epstein

My woman is sharper than new truth,
    a clean bullethole in thick glass.
Winter cuts its teeth on her, the sun
    cuts its hand on her,
She's too hot for the beach, the golden sand
    Goes all to white crystal under her.
She's too proud, the full moon is her mirror.
When she turns from me I see her face
    in the rolling window of heaven
and when she comes barefoot to my bedside,
holding a candle,
an elf skates on my heartstream.
Eager candle, milk my mind of treasons.
She's young and I want to fill her with my world.

Cullen,

Now you and I are twins. If you don't wear this jacket I'll kill you. Just make sure you don't pull on the pockets . . . Here too is my address and number in Florida AND the key to my house in Remsenberg. That's near Westhampton, out on Long Island. It's very beautiful there; almost too beautiful. The house is on a bay right smack in the middle of a bird sanctuary. The family who owned it before me named it 'The Laughing Hat' and it's an appropriate name. It always makes me feel good to be there, which isn't very often nowadays. I've written the address below. Lots of addresses today. Please go on and use it whenever you like. Knowing you're there would make me very happy. Please be sure to leave dirty glasses in the sink so I know you were there. I'm serious!

I don't know about you, but as far as I'm concerned, this thing between us isn't over yet. Not by a long-shot. You must have hit me with some kind of wonder-fist because I *cannot* stop thinking about you. Even now.

This is what I wrote back to Florida:

Weber, thank you *very* much for the world's most beautiful jacket. I've never had anything like it. I don't know what to say other than I'll take good care of it. Your kindness is unfairly huge. I don't think I'll ever use your 'Laughing Hat' house, but I like having the key on my ring.

I looked at the note and changed the punctuation around twenty times. Then I threw it in the waste-basket and went in to make dinner.

Danny and I had had a fight. A middle-of-the-winter, we're-bored-and-there's-nothing-better-to-do-so-let's-annoy-each-other fight. Danny was sort of right and so was I. Who cares? It ended with me walking regally out of the room.

'I'm going to bed!'

Luckily I had put the baby down half an hour before our fireworks started. Luckily the bathroom was connected to the bedroom, so I didn't have to lose face by seeing my husband again on my way to wash up. It was only nine o'clock, but I had no other alternative but bed.

The dream began in an empty room which reminded me of a ballet rehearsal hall. Middle-aged women in nondescript dresses stood in the centre of the room; there must have been twenty of them in all and they had identical long green scarves in their hands, which they swept across the floor in slow choreographed arcs. The end of each scarf was on fire, but the flame didn't grow or consume the silk; it flickered on each end like a lit wick.

The women stared blankly at me. The air in the room was heavy and rank with smoke and old sweat. The scarves burned in queer, alien colours.

'You don't live here any more. Your name is James!' They said it as one, and their stiff unison was unnerving. 'You have no right to the Bones. You live *away!*'

They started moving towards me, scarves behind them. Glaring tails.

'Stay here and your Mae burns. Little scarf. Silken baby.'

Our dreams are like the messes children make in a kitchen when no one is around to yell at them. Ketchup, an egg or two, chocolate sauce—all thrown into a blender and zipped around.

Where's the wheatgerm and look at that tin of clams! Throw 'em in! A little from real life, a few daydreams, a lot from God-knows-where, and *voilà!* There was the movie for the night. But with the advent of my special, strange Rondua, things had grown increasingly more clear, connected and sometimes frightening.

I woke. It was only the second time a reference had been made in the dreams to my real waking world, but in both cases it had had to do with Mae.

I slid out of bed as quietly as possible and walked into the livingroom. The little light over her crib was on for some reason and she was lying on her back, wide awake. It must have been three in the morning.

'Hello, Mommy.'

'Mae?'

Five months old and she had said my name.

'Yes, Mommy, I was waiting for you.'

Gripping the side of the crib, I stared down at her.

'Go look at your face, Mommy. The women did it. They scare me so much. They *burn.*'

The next thing I knew, I was standing in front of the bathroom mirror staring at my brand-new face. Coloured swirls and circles, blue flecks, a small black horse were all drawn over my forehead and cheeks, chin . . . I touched myself here and there to make sure. The skin, as if to confirm its change, was slick and slimy. The little horse over my right eye blurred for ever under my unbelieving, sliding fingers. The purple circle became a cone, the indigo . . .

I woke and this time the world was the real mine: Danny right next to me, his back curved and warm and totally familiar, the pillow under my head, the Italian alarm clock offensive in its solid electronic beeping.

'Holy Cow! You again?'

The telegram man looked disgustedly at me and held out another one. 'Just doing the job, lady. What'd you do, win the lottery or something?'

He had been there four times that day. The three previous telegrams had been from Weber Gregston and all said the same thing: 'Today I'm missing you more than I ever thought possible. Please punch me again.'

Two weeks earlier I'd had a bunch of postcards from Florida where he was scouting locations for a new film. For no good reason, he'd spent a weekend taking a train across the state. Getting off at stations all along the way, he sent me postcards from places like DeFuniak Springs, Cornbee Settlement and Mary Esther.

I walked back into the living-room and waved this newest telegram at Eliot. He had dropped by for an afternoon piece of cake.

'*Another* one? Oh, Cullen, they're going to have you in *Interview* magazine: "Who is the mysterious Gregston's mysterious paramour?" I *love* it!'

'Oh, shut up! Eliot, what's he up to?'

'I would say he's trying to get you, but in a very romantic way. If it had been me, I'd have been his after the leather jacket. Now I think he likes your stubbornness. Have you written back?'

'Not a word.'

'Has he called you? Come on, cut me a bigger piece, Cullen. You're always such a tightwad.'

'He hasn't called me since that time we went to the market. The telegrams are daring enough, thank you. What's the scoop on him, Eliot? Is he a big wolf? How can a man be so vile the first time you meet and then so sweet after that? Is he schizo?'

'I checked on it for you, Cullen. I think he's just tremendously shy and guarded. A lot of people come at him from all angles, so he retreats into an easy corner—he snarls. There are a lot of movie people who use that device, believe me. The news I had on him is interesting. For a few years he lived with a writer named Lenore Conroy. Word has it that she left him for someone else, but that there were no hard feelings between them at the end. The women who know him well enough all say basically the same thing—he's reliable, thoughtful and a very good friend to have.

'Cullen, there's something I've got to tell you I've been thinking about. Remember how he said he couldn't stop thinking about you only *after* you'd knocked him down? I don't want to scare you or anything, but do you think maybe a little Rondua has crossed over into his life?'

'Oh swell! Thanks, Eliot. There aren't enough problems around here! Now I'm going to start thinking I've got magical *powers!*'

Eliot put a piece of cake in his mouth and shrugged. 'It's just a thought.'

'Yeah, but what if you're right?'

The front door slammed and Danny called in to us that he was home. Eliot and I looked quickly at each other, as if we had been caught by our parents doing something very naughty. Well, we had.

94

Danny knew nothing about Weber Gregston, purple light, the dream of the women with the fiery scarves. Eliot snatched the telegrams off the coffee table and I slid the one in my hand into my pocket.

Danny came in and dropped down on the sofa next to me. Startled as I was, I was still glad to see him. His presence in a room always lifted me a little.

'Hiya, kids! How many pieces of cake has Eliot had? Cul, I've got some interesting news for you. Has a guy from the police called you yet? A guy named Flossmann?'

'*Flossmann?* I remember him; he questioned me after Alvin Williams killed his family. Why would he be calling us now?'

Eliot got up. 'Should I go?'

Danny shook his head and gestured for him to sit down again. 'No. Actually, it's all pretty interesting. And you stop jumping to conclusions, Cullen. I got a call this morning from your detective Flossmann. He said Alvin Williams is requesting permission to write to you.'

'Axe Boy wants to write to me? What for?'

'Oh Cullen, you lucky *thing!* Axe Boy never writes to *me!*'

'Shut up, Eliot! Why does Alvin Williams want to write to me, Dan?'

Both men wore full, shit-eating grins on their pusses. When they looked at each other across my discomfort, the grins widened appreciably.

'Cut it out! This isn't a joke, is it?' I glared at Danny, waiting for an answer. He shook his head. 'All right then, a lot of protection you two guys will be when the going gets tough!'

Danny took my hand, trying the whole time to bite the smile off his lips from inside. Across the room Mae came awake and Eliot went for her.

'Flossmann said you were the only one who was ever nice to him, Cul—at least, that's what Alvin says. He wants to write and thank you. I guess it's also because he's lonely.'

'Lonely and loony! Uh-uh! I've got enough problems, Danny. Give me that baby, Eliot.'

Standing behind Danny, Eliot was able to get away with mouthing 'Weber Gregston' without being seen. Then he danced Mae around in a circle.

'You know where *I* was when he killed his mother? In the laundry room, doing a white wash. By the time I came upstairs again, everyone interesting had left. Typical me!'

'Danny, why did the cop call you if I'm supposed to get the letter?'

'Because he was afraid the idea would upset you. He wanted to know if you were the nervous type.'

'Nervous type? Me? Not me! Hi, Axe Boy! You wanna play with my daughter?'

'Cullen, you don't have to say yes.'

'Of course I do, Danny. That's a lesson I learned from you, pal.'

'You remember that song we heard the other day? "You've got to kick at the darkness till it bleeds daylight"?'

'Danny, whenever I kick something I hurt my foot.'

The first letter arrived on a Monday, along with another postcard from Weber. I read the card first, so that I'd have a nice feeling before I leapt into the dark soup of Alvin Williams land. What a pair of pen-pals!

> Cullen,
>   I met a Countess von So-and-So today who's interested in financing my next film. I don't understand why people are so delighted to find that one of their ancestors was a Duke or a Count. All it means is a long time ago somebody did something horrible to someone else and was rewarded for it by some monstrous or syphilitic king.
>   Here's a quote I came across today that made me think of you: 'As long as I know that you understand,' he whispered. 'But of course you do. It's a great satisfaction to have got somebody to understand. You seem to have been there on purpose.' And in the same whisper, as if we two whenever we talked had to say things to each other which were not fit for the world to hear, he added, 'It's very wonderful.' It's from Conrad's *The Secret Sharer*.
>   I've given you my address here twice. Are you ever going to write?

I scratched my head and flirted with the idea of sending him back a postcard with the word 'No' written on it.

I put my hand on the letter from Williams and pushed it back and forth across the desk. The address had been written with a typewriter, which somehow made everything more cold and creepy. How could an axe murderer very calmly sit down and plunk out a letter on a typewriter? The careful spacing and precision of the letters and sentences all in sharp black order were so much the opposite of what he had done to his poor mother and sister.

On the other hand, I realized I had no desire to see the actual handwriting of this person. That would have been more naked and distressing, maybe even obscene.

Dear Mrs James,

It was very nice of you to allow me to write to you like this. But I've heard there are autograph collectors out there in the world who pay a lot of money for letters from people like me. What you can do is *sell* them this letter after you've read it a couple of times. Buy your daughter Mae a toy with the money. Just make sure to tell her it comes partly from her friend Alvin Williams! Ha ha!

I've been thinking about that day when we met on the street in front of our house. Do you remember? It was cloudy and sunny, back and forth all day long. You looked really great that day, Mrs James! You can't imagine how good I felt standing there talking to you. Everyone watched us when they walked by. Mr James is a very lucky man to have you as his wife. You're one of the most beautiful women I've ever seen, but one of the things I like so much about you is you never show off about it. You're warm and friendly. You always had time to talk with me whenever we met up with each other. I always hoped I'd meet you on the stairs. I bet you didn't know that, did you? I have to go now. I'll write to you again soon.

Very sincerely yours,
Alvin Williams

'Danny, do you think we'll need chains?'

'Cullen, honey, we're just driving to your parents' house, not Siberia.'

'I know, but I worry.'

'Yes, I noticed . . .'

Eliot sat in the back seat with Mae on his lap. 'Cullen, will you please get in? Your husband will take very good care of us. If you ever let him.'

I sighed and opened the car door. The sky was slush grey and threatened all kinds of snow. It had been my bright idea to round up the gang and spend a weekend at my parents' house on Long Island, but now I wasn't so thrilled. I envisioned bullying snowdrifts and silvery iced roads way out there in the wilds, where no one in their right mind *ever* went before May 1.

Typical me. It hadn't snowed in the city since March had arrived two weeks before. Winter's cold was still around, but the days lived longer and Mae woke at six each morning because the light was everywhere in the apartment by then.

I put my hand on the back of Danny's neck and twirled his hair around my finger. 'Did I turn the stove off?'

He smiled and put the car in gear. His hair was longer than ever and his face was full of mischief. It was hard to believe that a year before, we were living in Milan without a child and my husband was making hook-shots for a living.

The ride out of town was on pleasantly empty roads that welcomed our company all the way out past the two airports and on to the Long Island expressway.

Whenever I travelled this route, I remembered trips with my parents as a girl. Already in my swimsuit as the car pulled out of Manhattan, I would perch like a parrot between the folks' seats and keep up a two-hour running commentary on exactly what I would do when we got to the house. My mother would tell me not to breathe on Daddy's neck, while Dad would point out licence plates from exotic states like Wyoming and North Dakota.

Danny and Eliot chatted while I looked out of the window, feeling warm and complete. My husband, baby and best friend were all there and all mine for a couple of days. Weather fears aside, I knew we would have fun. We'd go into Southampton one day and feel like natives for a few hours by walking around the deserted streets. The store windows would be full of inappropriately bright things, hibernating there until the flashy summer crowd returned and started whipping out their credit cards.

What else would we do? Build big fires in the living-room fireplace, cook marshmallows on sticks. Mae had never seen a marshmallow. For that matter, she'd never seen a fire! Oh sure, a second's match flick here and there, but never a luxuriously big blast of yellow and heat dancing off red brick. No sir, never that! It was about time.

'I'm hungry.'

'Danny, we haven't even got to Port Jefferson yet!'

'Cullen, please reach down and hand me a large sandwich, pickle and a can of cream soda. I'm hungry, there's a basket full of food and if you want to have an argument with my stomach—go right ahead.'

'I guess that's touché to you, toots!'

'Pipe down, Eliot. You can't have any food anyway. Hello, Mae darling. Would *you* like a sandwich?'

There was snow on the ground by the time we passed the sign for Westhampton, the exit you would take if you were going to Weber Gregston's house. How did I know that? Because I looked it up on a map before we left, that's how. I watched the sign approach, get larger and larger, flick by. Weber. Was he in New York again? Did I want him to call me? See me? Eliot asked those questions this morning and I had had to shrug. No. Yes. No. Yes. Maybe.

But Eliot's interest in the Weber Gregston affair was purely academic because, next to me, he was Danny's greatest supporter. He would have been aghast if I had done anything about Weber besides fantasize. Yet I was still more honest with him about certain things than I was with Dan. Eliot heard every Rondua dream and seemed perpetually fascinated by them. He was now convinced they were an important part of my well-being. The E. Kilbertus analysis was that Cullen James was an interesting person who, at the moment, wasn't able to live up to her potential because of the humdrum busy work involved in taking care of an infant. As a result, I let my unconscious take off nightly and the adventures in Rondua compensated for the mundaneness of my everyday. That logical and highly complimentary view—coming from one who knew every detail of the situation—reassured me mightily. It also helped to know that what he said agreed essentially with what Dr Rottensteiner had told me months before: if the dreams didn't have any bad effects, just leave them alone. It reminded me of the dust motes that float around in front of our eyes; follow them with your eye and they remain in your vision much longer than if you ignore them and let them drift away.

And how about the time I realized with a hefty jolt how much I would *miss* those damned dreams if they were suddenly to go away? Anything that is wholly ours sets us apart from the rest of the universe.

Overall, the only thing that tickled my mind the wrong way was what in God's name had I done to Weber that day I put up my hand and sent him flying across his hotel room? That haunted me when I let myself think about it—which, believe me, was *not* often.

*

The first thing that struck me about my parents' house when we pulled into the driveway was how forlorn it looked: ready to be filled and have some fun with people moving around in its belly, turning up all the heat.

As we ferried back and forth to and from the car with all the bags and boxes we'd brought, Eliot pulled me aside out of Danny's earshot and said we *had* to make a safari over to Remsenberg one day to check out Villa Gregston. I agreed with a curt nod, but a white light of excitement clicked on in my heart as I did so. I know I wouldn't have gone alone, but how could I say no with Eliot *insisting*. . . .

The first night out on the Island, Eliot whipped up his family's secret bean soup which we ate from hot bowls by the fireplace along with thick chunks of cheese and homemade bread and a good French red wine. Mae was transfixed by the fire, but very blasé about the marshmallows we toasted for her. She fell asleep with a fat black one in her hand, but we kept her there with us to complete our circle as we sat around, dreaming and not saying much.

The next afternoon, Danny said there was a Rutgers basketball game on television he wanted to see. He volunteered to babysit if Eliot and I wanted to go out and wander around.

With that perfect excuse to sneak over to Weber's house, I suddenly had no desire to go. But Eliot piped up and loudly announced his willingness to be chauffeured around and shown all the interesting sights in the neighbourhood.

An hour later we were half-way there, feeling like ten-year-olds who were sneaking into an 'R' rated movie without their parents along.

It was love at first sight for me and Remsenberg. White wooden houses hundreds of years old sat quietly next to each other in that proud, justifiable arrogance old beauty often has.

There was no real town centre—no stores or gas stations. Only the houses simply but perfectly maintained, very sure of their great value. What an uncommon place.

An old man in a plucky Tam O'Shanter hat who was walking a sweet-faced greyhound gave us directions to the lane where Weber lived. Turning on to it and feeling my hands go a little sweaty, I was reminded of those roads in rural Italy that are lined on either side by cypress trees which commonly give you the feeling they're soldiers waiting to be reviewed. Only here on Long Island, there were cedar

100

trees with a solid, rocky look to them which said they had stood
guard over this part of town for a long time.

The road twisted here and there. Finally, after a strangely sharp
right turn, it became a narrow dirt road. I pulled the car over and we
both got out to have a look. Sure enough, Eliot found the mailbox a
few feet away under a tree with the name 'Gregston' written under
it in small, unobtrusive letters.

'Eliot, I think we should walk in, don't you? If he is in there, we
don't want to surprise him. What if he's with someone, or something?'

'And maybe you're scared stiff, Cullen James. Where's your spirit
of adventure?'

'In Rondua, Mr Tracy. Let's go.'

The driveway meandered in and out of a neat, very thick forest of
trees and was only wide enough for one car at a time. It went on for
about a quarter of a mile. Then you were socked in the eye with *one
beautiful view!* Weber's 'Laughing Hat' house sat plunk on the edge of
a bay and fitted perfectly into the surroundings of sea and birds
flying everywhere. It was a little Victorian gem, white and cobalt
blue, which reminded me of a Carl Larson illustration for a children's book. Every detail was singular and kooky—gingerbread
moulding, orange copper drains, giant bay windows that gave the
impression the house was all eyes looking carefully out at everything.

There was no car around. Tiptoeing up closer, we saw no lights on
inside either.

'Damn it! I wanted him to be in there with Meryl Streep.'

'Meryl's married, Eliot.'

'Frankly, my dear, so are you. You want to go inside? You've got
the keys, right?'

'Yes, but I don't want to do that, Eliot. I feel voyeuristic enough as
it is.'

'Oh my! I've been a peeping Tom all my life. There's just never
anything very interesting to peep *at!* Are you sure? Can you imagine
what he's got hidden in those closets?'

'No, I really don't want to. But I think we can peek in through the
windows. That'd be okay.'

We made a complete circuit of the house. Since so much of it was
glass, we got a good idea of his taste from out there. There were lots
of empty white walls, wooden furniture covered with black silk

pillows, some posters of work by artists I'd never heard of before but liked a lot: Leslie Baker, Alex Colville, Martina Niegel. And there was no one 'kind' of picture or theme—they were as eclectic as you could get.

Neatly arranged on the low ebony living-room table were big art books and a copy of the Italian men's *Vogue* magazine with guess who on the cover? Weber Gregston. What I couldn't see, Eliot described to me, and vice versa. After a while I felt like a relative who's come to take stock of things after a member of the family has died.

'Tell me you're *sure* you don't want to go in.'

'Eliot—'

'Okay, I was just asking. But let's leave him something to let him know you were here. Remember how he said he'd like that?'

Neither of us had a pen or paper, so a note was out. Eliot suggested we make a little pile of stones at the door, but that reminded me too much of a Jewish cemetery.

'Wait a minute. I know.' I fished down deep into my purse and came up with the last postcard Weber had sent from Florida. There was a brass mail slot on the front door and I shoved the card through it.

'Maybe he'll just think you didn't like what he said on the card, Cullen. Let's go in and write him a real note.'

'Come on, Eliot. You'd just steal something if you went in.'

It was dark when we got back home and Danny was lying on the couch reading a book. Mae was sitting on the floor hitting her favourite stuffed animal—an ugly green squirrel—with a plastic spoon.

'Hallo!'

'Where have you two been? I was beginning to worry.'

'Oh, we drove around! All over the place. I took Eliot to Westhampton . . . I'm sorry, Dan. We should have called.'

'Yes, that's right. What are we going to do about dinner?'

The tone of his voice and the snip of the words sent Eliot and me scuttling off pronto into the kitchen to get things going.

A few minutes later Danny poked his head around the corner to say he was going out to the store to buy some brownies.

'But Dan, we've already got . . .'

His eyes told me to be quiet; he wanted to go away from us for a while, and *not* just into another room of the house. I wished we hadn't gone to Weber's, no matter how much fun we'd had casing the place out. When Danny James went out for brownies at six in the evening, it meant he was angry as hell and didn't want to be around his wife. It also wrung my heart to realize he was mad because he'd been worried.

I waited until I heard the car door slam and the engine start up before I dared to look out of the kitchen window. I felt Eliot's hands on my shoulders as he leaned over me to have a look too.

'We're such little shits, Cullen.'

'Boy, don't I know it!'

'Can you imagine how he'd feel if he knew where we'd really been? Oh, my God!'

'Spare me. Let's just go and make a *very* beautiful dinner and pray he comes back in one piece. He hasn't done something like this since we were in Italy.'

I brought Mae in from the living-room and put her in the highchair. Then we set to work making a king's feast. Eliot started to sing 'Can't Help Loving That Man of Mine' but stopped dead as soon as he saw the look on my face.

Danny's return half an hour later was marked by two sighs of relief from the kitchen, but no hugs and kisses all around. He walked into the kitchen, put a bag on the counter and walked out again.

I looked into the bag and my heart broke all over again. Next to some frozen brownies was the newest issue of my favourite magazine. Damn him! Damn all good people who make you feel so keenly aware of your own smallness, ineptitude and spite with the flick of their wrist or an unconscious blink of the eye.

I wanted to run into the living-room waving my spatula, to yell at him, 'Why do you have to be so damned nice? You make me feel one foot tall!'

But I didn't do that; I turned the potato pancakes over instead.

Our dinner was eaten in silence; the final nail being driven into the day's coffin when Dan insisted on doing all the dinner dishes.

Eliot and I went into the living-room and sat looking helplessly at each other.

'Maybe there's a Weber Gregston movie on TV.'

There was a tremendous crash in the kitchen and Danny yelled, 'Mae, don't!'

He had dropped the casserole dish on the floor and, fast as only a child can be when it's interested in something, Mae picked up a fanged piece of broken glass that had landed on her chair.

When I got there, the shard had bit deep into her silly putty hand and there was blood all over . . . All over everything. Mae looked at the red gush interestedly—it was something new for her.

Danny saw me bolt for her and threw up his hand to stop me in my charge. 'Don't scare her, Cul! Do it slow. If you scare her it'll be worse!'

Perfect sense. My face went through six changes while I took slow giant steps towards her.

'Good job, kiddo! Let me have a look.' I could feel the hysteria rise inside me like vomit.

The cut was very deep. A gut-sickening gash that had no end.

'What should we do, Dan?'

'Oh, my *God!*'

That did it. Eliot's whoop on first seeing what had happened scared the hell out of Mae and the whole thing exploded right there. Mae started to scream.

'Eliot, shut up and call the operator! Tell her what's happened and ask for the nearest emergency service or doctor. Whichever one is closer.'

Eliot stood unmoving in the doorway, his hands pressed to his mouth.

'For Christ's sake move, Eliot! Cullen, get her over here. Let me try and clean it up.'

Out of the corner of my eye I saw Eliot disappear. I lifted the blood-ribboned Mae up and out of her wooden high-chair.

Danny took hold of her at the sink. The first thing he did was lift her up so she was right at eye level with him. He gave her a big smile and wiggled his eyebrows.

'Hey baby, what a hand! Look at all of that great blood! Let's wash it off a little, huh?'

Seeing her Daddy smile calmed her a little, but the screams soon returned when he began rinsing the hand in cold tap water.

'Cul, go get a clean handkerchief or something; anything, a rag. Just make sure it's clean. I'm going to try to make a bandage.'

Eliot blasted through the door with the name of a doctor a mile away.

'Go call him. See if he's home.'

'No, let's just go, Danny. We'll waste—'

'No! If he's not there, we'll just have to come back here again. Call him!'

The doctor wasn't home, but his answering machine gave the name of someone else. That doctor *was* home and told us to come right over. He would be waiting for us.

Danny wrapped her hand and then carefully bound it at the wrist with a rubber band from my hair.

When we got in the car, Mae was really on the edge of something bad. The pain had obviously arrived and she didn't like one bit the shift we'd made from warm house to cold car.

Danny told me to drive because I knew the way. He sat next to me with Mae on his lap, jiggling her up and down and singing little songs in her ear.

In the back seat, Eliot asked if there was anything he could do.

'Yes, sing. Let's all sing a song. Mae likes it when we sing, don't you, Kiwi?'

I looked at Danny and loved him for everything he had in him: all the stores of strength and sanity I knew from our everydays together, and all the extra parts he had for moments like this, when coolness and clarity were the only things that mattered.

Eliot started singing. Unfortunately. He didn't stop singing until we were getting out of the car in front of the doctor's house.

Later, when the doctor told us we had bound Mae's hand a little too tightly, I felt like telling him to . . . My husband had wrapped that hand and nothing he did could be wrong.

'Mom, this is Night Ear. He'll show us around.'

We stood at the gates of another city that looked so much like Kempinski: the same turrets, campaniles, mobs of black birds flying to and fro over the high stone walls. We were outside Ophir Zik, the City of the Dead. I knew nothing about it except that I didn't like anything about its name.

When we left Kempinski days before, Pepsi had climbed on to Mr Tracy's head and they moved off ahead of us. I assumed it was because they had important things to talk about, but that assumption didn't make things any easier. Pepsi was still a very little boy and even in mystical Rondua, where rabbits pulled magicians out of their top hats, I felt it was just too soon for this not-even-three-foot-tall fellow to begin assuming the responsibilities of a man, much less those of a monarch.

But then again he wouldn't be a monarch unless he possessed all five Bones. So far he had got only two, and one of those old unnecessary Mom had found for him.

More and more, I asked myself what function did I serve here? Somehow, from some*where,* I had come to Rondua with Pepsi. Was I therefore a messenger, meant only to deliver my dream-child to the right people here and then be gone? No, because of everything that had happened so far: I had had to introduce him to the animals, I had had to explain certain things about Rondua to him, I had helped calm his initial fears about being there in the first place. Then *I* had found the first Bone of the Moon and shown my son how to carve it. So, was I just a messenger? Maybe I was fooling myself, but I was sure it was much more than that. But what? Since Pepsi had been treated so respectfully by Sizzling Thumb and the mayor of Kempinski, I had felt increasingly left out of things and more like an unnecessary part than ever.

Once it even struck me that if I had to stay in Rondua longer, it would be better for me to go back to the Plain of Forgotten Machines and hang around with them. I'd fit right in with those things —I could splutter and hiss importantly and serve no purpose at all. Just like those other pretty heaps we'd passed on that day so many weeks before.

Why do brats like me like to lick our wounds so much?

Night Ear was an old hermit who chose to live on the outskirts of Ophir Zik. He made his small living by showing visitors around the City of the Dead.

'The ones who live inside are comfortable with each other. But they resent the living, so it's best not to talk with them. However, if you must, look away. Don't look them in the face, and address your questions to no one directly. They'll know who you are talking to.'

We followed him through a ruined arched gate. The cobblestone path that led into the city gradually steepened upward. Soon my legs were tired and I found myself taking smaller steps and watching my feet to make sure they were going where I wanted them to.

Children ran helter-skelter through the wobbly, uneven streets, but their happy laughing faces made no noise. Nothing. There was no noise anywhere. Not the shouts of children, dogs barking, the bang of buckets and metal on stone, the squawks of birds or people saying hello across a narrow alleyway.

Women in colourful babushkas with their sleeves rolled up and faces red as children's candy leaned out of their windows and watched interestedly as we passed. But they watched in silence too: old hens as nosy in mute death as they had been in loud life. To my surprise, one of them threw an apple down to me. It was shiny and delicious looking, but it made no sound when it landed in my hand. I looked at Night Ear to see if it was all right to eat. He waited until we had rounded a sharp corner and were out of view of the woman.

'It's not a good idea to eat that; it'll only make you tired.' He stopped and looked at me craftily. 'But you *can* eat it, if you want. If you do, it will tell you many things about death you never knew.'

A young good-looking man rode slowly by on a bicycle with his girl-friend balanced on the bar in front of him, her hands tightly over his on the handlebars. They were both smiling and looked as if they couldn't have been happier. But they made no sound. The bicycle shuddered and bumped over the old grey-brown stones, but it made no sound and they were soon gone.

It was more odd than frightening. I had almost grown used to the quiet when we came upon a sunny wide-open plaza and I saw Evelyn Hernuss, Danny's first wife, sitting at a café and watching us. Forgetting what the guide had said, I hurried over and—looking directly at her—said her name.

'Hello, Cullen. We're not allowed to shake hands with you. How many years has it been, though? You've done so much since I knew you.'

We spoke for a few minutes about . . . what? My marrying Danny. She knew all about that. She said it was 'okay', that she was happy for both of us, but the look on her face—so full of stopped dreams and sadness—said it wasn't okay at all. What could I do or say? For a brief moment, I felt as if I had killed her and sent her here.

'Mom?'

I looked down at Pepsi without really seeing him. He was crying. I looked from him to Evelyn, and then back again at him. His face was wet, but he kept nodding at me as if he were agreeing with something I had said.

'Why are we here, Pepsi?' I looked again from him to Evelyn, then back again.

107

'Don't you know?'

'Not at all, my love.'

'You have to! This is where I was before you came back, Mom. I lived here. You killed me once. Don't you remember that?'

A pain the size of the world swept through me and to this day, I have no idea whether it was physical or spiritual or what. What I do know is that death itself could not be any worse than that pain. Nothing could.

Pepsi was the child I had had scraped out of me four years before on a sunny summer day. My abortion. My son. Getting rid of my evidence. My son—my dead, wonderful son.

Leaning my whole sagged weight against a wall, I wept again in the midst of that dreadful silence for what I had done. I wept until I felt crushed by the weight of both the world and the dead.

I had been wondering why I was in Rondua. But not once had I ever really wondered about the identity of this beautiful, sassy child who had gone everywhere with me and called me Mom. My son. My son here, my son from the other world.

I was in Rondua for only one reason: to help Pepsi however I could to find the five Bones of the Moon and thus keep him from this city for the rest of time.

Why we were both being given this second chance I had no idea, but it was there and I would ask no questions. Without the Bones, Pepsi would be here forever. With them, he would be free, he would be able to streak across mountains on Martio the Camel's back or swim by himself in gold lagoons. I was here this time not to find the Bones myself, but to help Pepsi home . . . Through and out of Ophir Zik, the City of the Dead, to life somewhere on the far other side of this universe.

Does it ever really happen that we are given a *real* second chance? Another turn to bat, a few magical feet more to skid before we hit the wall and ruin everything?

No, in real life that didn't happen. In Rondua, I would save my child.

PART THREE

PART THREE

1

Dear Mrs James,

Dr Lavery says I am making good progress. I don't exactly know what he means by that, but I'll have to take his word for it.

In the meantime, I have been reading all the time and have tentatively decided to become a veterinarian when I am released from here. Not that I expect *that* to happen any time soon! I don't think they understand me very well here. They pretend to listen to what I am saying, but I see their eyes looking at other places when I am talking. I never thought of doctors being dishonest. There's not many people you can trust these days, are there? I must say though that I think I can trust you. That is why I am writing to you. I hope you don't mind too much.

My favourite books so far are those popular best-sellers about a veterinarian working in England. You know, the ones that have been turned into the very successful television series on the educational channel? Personally, I don't watch the show itself because I think television is for idiots. There are many big colour television sets here at the Institute which are turned on all day long. It is almost impossible to avoid the noise they make, no matter where you are or what you are doing.

I'm sure all of my letters to you are monitored and read by someone here, and they will most likely raise an eyebrow at the animosity exhibited by my attitude, but I do not mean it to sound that way. I only wish to plead the case of turning those infernal sets *down*. That isn't too much to ask, is it? Not everyone here is interested in re-runs of the 'Superman' show, believe me! There are those of us who are interested in more important things. Personally I would only like a quiet corner somewhere where I could read, or simply think, but often even that is virtually impossible to find in this overly-loud place.

Oh, well, one can't have everything one wants in life.

111

How are you and Mr James? Healthy and happy, I sincerely hope. Is your child Mae talking yet? In your last letter you mentioned her age, so I went to the library here and spent a good few hours reading up on the subject. Did you know that it is not uncommon for children to begin speaking at a surprisingly early age? Listen carefully—those funny baby sounds you hear may even be the real thing!

Well, that's all for now. I hope I haven't bored you too much this time. As I seem to tell you every time, I think a great deal about what I want to say to you in these letters. Somehow they never turn out to sound like I want them to, or say the right thing.

Oh well, I said that I wanted to be a veterinarian and not a writer, so I guess that's okay. Ha! Ha!

I will write again in a few days, you poor woman.

Very sincerely yours,
Alvin Williams

Dear Alvin,

Thank you for your last letter. What you said about when children begin to talk was interesting, but I'm afraid our little Mae is still at the stage where the four words in her entire vocabulary are all variations of either oogle or google.

I think your idea about becoming a veterinarian is a good one. My husband suggested you might want to look into different correspondence courses that are offered by certain schools. I don't know if you have your high school diploma yet, but it might be worthwhile to investigate this possibility. That way, you could gain certain credits while you are in the Institute and then continue your studies later at whatever school has the course you want.

When I was at college, I never had any real idea of what I wanted to do with my life later. As a result, I took courses all over the place in only the things that interested me. It was nice and I ended up with a degree in history, but in retrospect it was not a terrifically productive way of going about things. I admire your being able to tell even now what it is you want later.

A veterinarian does a great job. My good friend Eliot Kilbertus says he only wishes he could find a good one in New York. According to him, they all charge a fortune but aren't very effective.

The spring seems to have arrived and I'm glad of it. Recently all of us went out to Long Island for the weekend. A friend of mine owns a house out there in Remsenberg, right in the middle of a bird sanctuary. When we went there I noticed that some of the frailer fellows had already flown in from wintering down south, and it's not even the middle of the month yet. A good sign. I even had a dream the other night where I was walking around in a teeshirt and the ugliest Bermuda shorts you ever saw. When you start dreaming about shorts, summer can't be too far off.

Be well.

Cullen James

2

'Cullen?'

'Yes?'

'Where did you get this leather jacket? It is beautiful!'

My eyebrows went straight up while my eyes closed tight. Weber Gregston's leather jacket! I'd hidden it in the deepest, darkest corner of my closet and *never* wore it when Danny was around. He was very aware of what I wore and almost always noticed when I had on something new. I'd figured out that if I waited a few months, then one day I could casually tell him about this *incredible* bargain I'd picked up at a thrift shop right down the block . . .

The best-laid plans of mice and men . . .

'What jacket?'

'This one—the leather one.' He came into the room holding it out in front of him. 'Where the hell did you get this? It's fantastic!'

'Uh oh. Discovery time. Don't get mad.'

'Mad? Cul, you didn't charge it, did you? Honey, I know you love clothes and as far as I'm concerned when we have the money—'

'No, Danny, wait! I didn't charge it. Eliot gave it to me for my birthday.'

'Your birthday? That's not for a month!'

I shrugged—little Miss Innocent. 'Yes, well, he gave it to me early, Dan. What am I supposed to say? We knew you'd squawk about it and that's why I didn't tell you. Are you mad?'

'Cullen, I assume "Gianni Versace" means it's Italian. Italian leather jackets cost more than the national debt. I don't care how rich Eliot is; this is just too much.'

I watched him walk to the phone, call my excuse and ask him to come over to our apartment for a few minutes.

114

'Hi, guys! Oh good, you both look pissed off. Are you fighting? Can I watch?'

'Eliot, did you really give this jacket to Cullen for her birthday?'

'No.' His face was blank.

'Eliot!' My voice got very close to cracking. 'Don't lie! Tell the truth. You did too give it to me for my birthday.'

'No, I didn't, Cullen. I gave it to you because I love you. Your birthday just happened to be a good excuse.'

My blood pressure dropped several notches, but not Danny's. He handed me the jacket and sat down next to me on the couch, frowning all the while. 'El, you can't do that!'

'Daniel, old chum, I happen to have something exquisite for your birthday too. Would you like me to go down and get it?'

'No, Eliot. Now you're making me feel very uncomfortable. It's not right; it's really nice of you, but the whole thing's not right.'

'That's true, but this way you'll both feel completely indebted and guilty if you don't treat me wonderfully.'

'Oh come on, Danny. You're generous yourself. Don't make Eliot feel bad just because he is too.'

For the first time in our lives together, my husband threw his hands in the air. 'That's not the point, Cullen. I'm not Ebenezer Scrooge!'

'God bless our presents, every *one!*'

'Quiet, Eliot! You know exactly what I'm talking about.'

'Danny, since I'm the accused here, I have a right to say something. The James family are the only people on the entire face of the earth I would do *anything* for. And you both know that. Anything! Everyone else I hang around with is witty, charming and full of shit. All gleam and no stuff. I love some of them, hate most and trust no one but the two of you. That's the truth. If you stopped being my friends, I'd die!

'The truth of the matter is, I made out my will six weeks ago because my lawyer was being annoying. I made Mae the beneficiary. I'm worth a little over four hundred thousand dollars. I wouldn't trust either of you thieves with it, but my god-daughter is going to go to Radcliffe if she likes. Neither of you has my permission to protest or even talk about it. *Basta.* Period.'

I looked at him and gave a very crooked smile. 'Aw, Eliot, you old . . .'

Danny got up and embraced him. They held on to each other a

115

good long time while I watched, clutching the forgotten leather jacket in my hands.

I had once thought strength of character was a hardening of oneself; an intricate protection system by which you reconciled yourself to the truths of life and learned not to let them bother you. But all systems of character building go right out of the window when you find there aren't any more truths . . . or none you recognize.

After the incident with the jacket, I was very afraid to tell Danny what had happened with Weber Gregston and the new goings-on in Rondua. For the first time in our relationship, I began to doubt my husband and I truly hated that. I doubted him because he wasn't the person I wanted to confide in. Eliot, with his understanding of why people do naughty things sometimes, his sympathetic ear and whole-hearted belief in the unknown *was* the confidant I needed at that peculiar time in my life. I didn't want to close myself off or hide important things away from my husband, but I feared his lack of understanding. At best, he would sympathize. Eliot *empathized* and instead of pushing me towards having my head examined again, he wanted to examine that head with me and try to make sense of the whole mishmash of events and powers.

'Oh big deal, Cullen! So you had an abortion. *Everyone's* had an abortion; they're very old-hat. Even I had an abortion—my last lover, Judge Thompson.'

' "Judge"? That was his real name?'

'Yes, unfortunately. He was a small black man who wore a cowboy hat. He actually wanted me to buy him some spurs!'

'How come you never talk about your lovers, Eliot?'

'Because they all make me sad. I'm very unlucky in love. But I don't want to discuss them now. Do you see how right I was about this Rondua of yours? Everyone works out their troubles in their dreams. It's cheap analysis, you know? You had an abortion and you've felt horrible about it ever since. Somewhere in your mind you carried around this big bucket full of guilt, even though I think you're nuts to have done that. Anyway, with these Rondua dreams you're getting it out of your head. Great! Help that little Pepsi find the Bones of the Moon and you're home-free. How many have you got so far? Three?'

'Yes. The latest was the one for Fairness. Pepsi saved Felina's life and then let the Warm live.'

'What warm?'

'*The* Warm—that was its name. It danced on the desert and tried to eat Felina.'

'Felina's the wolf?'

'Right. And Martio's the camel, Mr Tracy's the dog—'

'—Who wears a black hat, right?'

'Right.'

The phone rang and Eliot got up to answer it. He spoke into the receiver a few seconds and then, surprisingly, held it out towards me with a very arch look on his face. 'It's your friend Weber Gregston, dearie. How did he know my number?'

I took hold of the phone as if it were a dangerous snake. 'Hello?'

'Hello, Cullen? Look, I'm sorry to call you there, but we *have* to talk. We have to.' His voice said he wasn't kidding around—it sounded tired and very strained.

'What's the matter, Weber? Are you okay?' I wanted to thank him for all the cards and telegrams and other things, but something more important was up.

'No, I'm not. We have to meet—like immediately? I just got into town and I have to talk with you. I'm not fucking around or anything, Cullen. Please don't be coy with me—something bad is happening and I think it's your fault. I'm sorry, but it's true. Can we get together now? Is that possible?'

Eliot, his head glued to mine, nodded vigorously. I pointed to the baby and he whispered that he would stay with her.

'Okay, Weber. Where are you?'

'At the phone-booth on your corner. Come down and we'll meet. Like, five minutes?'

'Okay. Hold tight and I'll be right down.'

I hung up and looked at Eliot. 'What do you think?'

'He didn't sound too good, Cullen.'

'I know. What do you think's wrong?'

'Not love this time. He was too shook up.'

Weber stood in front of our building. He looked as if he'd come back from the dark side of the moon.

'Holy cow, Weber! What *happened* to you?'

'That's what we're going to talk about. Where can we go?'

'Let's go to Lena's; it's just around the corner.'

He put both hands to his face and rubbed hard. His hair was wet and slicked back and his face was newly-shaven, but there were little red nicks all over it. 'I'm totally messed up. I haven't had a good night's sleep in a week.'

The restaurant was run by two nice women who served you heaps of good food and then left you alone. We sat at a table in the back, although it was late afternoon and the place was empty.

'What's up, Weber?'

He held up a hand to stop me. 'Wait. First let me ask you a couple of questions. Who are Pepsi and Mr Tracy?'

My head shot forward. 'How do you know about them? Who told you?'

'No one told me anything. I dream them, Cullen. Like, every *night* I dream about them! Pepsi, Mr Tracy and you. You most of all. What's going on, Cullen? Who are they? I'm telling you, I don't sleep so well any more. And you want to know when all this started? I figured it out the other night. It started right after I met you—after you knocked me down that day.'

'Tell me what you dream, Weber. Tell me exactly. Everything.'

'You know what I'm talking about, don't you?'

I felt a tension knot taking hold on the back of my neck. I remembered what Eliot had said about Weber being interested in me because I had 'enchanted' him the day we met.

'Yes, I know what you mean. Go on. Welcome to Rondua.'

'Rondua! That's right! That's the name, isn't it?'

We talked for three hours without stopping. I felt no hesitation in telling him everything: about the abortion, the beginning of my dreams, Pepsi, the search for the Bones, the City of the Dead.

We got hungry along the way and ordered two big lunches. Then around five o'clock, the restaurant began to fill up with the cocktail crowd. I called Eliot and told him I needed another hour. He said that was fine but what was happening?

'Weber has been dreaming around Rondua too. Ever since I zapped him in the chest.'

'Holy shit!'

'Uh-huh. I think you were right, Eliot. See you later. I'll tell you everything then.'

'Okay, I can't wait! Just don't zap anybody on your way home, huh?'

Weber had been places and met creatures in Rondua I didn't know —the alligator chess bullies, Cloud Hell, the night-time old lamp market in Harry. He'd been to the Caves of Lem and the Gardener's Office on the Mountain. One of the guides was a crane named A Sport and a Pastime. Later he was accompanied only by a voice named Solaris.

Neither of us could figure out why he had been in other corners of the land, but we agreed there was no sense in looking for logic in *any* of this. Why even try?

A little hesitantly, I told him Eliot's idea about how I had bewitched him the day we met.

He smiled and took a cold French fry off my plate. 'Why not, Cullen? It's just as crazy as everything else we've discussed.'

He took another French fry; he was calm now and smiling more, particularly when we talked about our different experiences over there.

Instead of eating the potato, he pointed it at me and began talking again. 'You know, it wouldn't be so bad if the damned dreams weren't so scary and upsetting. Have you met Jack Chili yet?'

'Jack who?'

'Jack Chili. Mama, you don't want to know him, *ever*. Look, lunch is over and we've got to figure this thing out now. I can't keep having these dreams, Cullen, no matter what's causing them. I don't even want to know especially how the hell they're happening. You touched me, hit me with that purple light and boom! I'm living in Rondua. Fine, I accept that; it's weird as hell, but I accept it. Now all I want to do is get out of there, that's all. Last night I dreamed about two guys blowing their heads off. Beautiful camera work: right up close with all the guts all over. Forget it; I can't have that any more.' He put down the potato and squashed it flat on to his plate with his fork. 'What should I do, Cullen? What can *you* do?'

'I think I know how to fix it.'

'You do? Are you serious? What?'

I told him the story of the confrontation with the machines on the plains. I told him about the word I used to get us out of that fix, and how in the dreams I knew I could use that word one more time to work its magic somewhere. Whether that magic carried over to a restaurant in New York City was something else.

'You can try, right? Say the word and let's see what happens.

Christ, I'm game for anything, Cullen! Anything to get them out of my head. Do it!'

I reached across the table and, with my flat hand against his forehead, said 'Koukounaries'.

He closed his eyes and put his hand on top of mine. 'Say it again.'

I did, but I was afraid to tell him that I felt no tingle or jive of magic go out of me, as it had on the day when the purple light had protected me.

Dear Mrs James,

Happy Birthday! I wrote Mr James a letter a while ago and asked him when your birthday was. Luckily I knew in time. I know this card is kind of dumb, but I had to ask one of the doctors to buy one for me, and this happened to be his taste. I should have known by the kind of neckties he wears that he wasn't the right man to ask! Ha, Ha! Anyway, happy birthday to you, happy birthday to you, happy birthday, Mrs James, happy birthday to you!

Very sincerely yours,
Alvin Williams

3

It was the first time we had seen the ocean since our arrival in
Rondua. It was pink and the waves, when they broke, frothed yellow. They were uncomfortable colours—childhood dreams gone
awry.

Pepsi stood by our 'boat'—an upside-down laughing fedora hat
the size of an old bath-tub. It was cold by the water—even my
shadow felt cold.

Weeks had passed since Kempinski, Ophir Zik and our battle
against the dancing Warm. Felina, saved by Pepsi there, died quietly
one night not long afterwards. Mr Tracy and Martio knew immediately and stood on either side of her body throughout the night.
Only at dawn did the giant black dog wake us by baying so sadly
and beautifully that it sounded like full notes played on an ancient
cello.

We didn't have to bury her because the body vanished as soon as
Pepsi placed the three Bones on her head, heart and left rear-leg. In
a few minutes only the Bones lay on the ground where she had slept
for the last time.

Martio said the winds would carry the dog's song back to the
wolf's family and they would know she was gone by the end of the
day.

The four of us continued our walk to the sea and missed her
gentle presence every day. A thought kept crossing my mind like an
important bulletin from some deeper part of me: 'There is no peace,
only rest.' I had no idea what it meant.

Ophir Zik was apparently the City of the Dead for human beings
here, but where did the other Ronduans go when they died? Intrigu-
ingly, that thought brought to mind another I had had as a little girl

121

and completely forgotten. If there was life on other planets and it was completely different from life on earth, where did those things go when *they* died? Or was heaven an Edward Hicks 'Peaceable Kingdom' where Earthlings ate with gook-eyed Martians and Ronduans lay down with dangerous creatures from Alpha Centauri?

There was time to think about these things because we had such a long way to go, all of it on foot now. The lands and things we saw there were as strange as ever—Jackie Billows in the Conversation Bath, a circus where memories performed—but in many ways Felina's death had emptied all of us and made us inured to wonder. One twilight we saw a lone dark horse galloping straight down a railway track at an oncoming train. At the last possible instant, the horse leapt gracefully into the air and took flight. None of us said anything.

The Slung People led us through the Caves of Lem and the wooden mice I had sung about so many months before guided us carefully over the Bridge of Art. We walked through a forest festooned with unmoving lightning bugs which Pepsi insisted on calling fire-bees. The next morning we woke at the bottom of a mile-wide crater that was black and phosphorescent green and steaming evilly everywhere.

Food was never a problem. We picked leos and sixhat wherever we found their blue groves, naletense by the side of rushing streams. It all tasted delicious, but I had forgotten long before to pay attention to what I put in my mouth. We ate when we had to, slept when exhaustion—like gravity—pulled us to the ground. We had to reach the Sea of Brynn before the moon's next eclipse, so we moved with the speed of secret couriers carrying messages of war from a king to his important generals.

I tired easiest and was often the one to call a halt to our flight. And flight it was, because Pepsi had only one chance to gain the fourth Bone of the Moon, which was somewhere in the immeasurable pink waters of the Sea of Brynn. What further complicated matters was the fact that it could only be done at night in the midst of a full lunar eclipse, with the stars our only guide.

Several days from our destination, we came to a remote cross-roads. Lying in the centre of it were eight dead rabbits, their bodies placed so as to form a macabre furred star. Without any prompting, Pepsi took the first Bone—the one he had carved into a walking stick—and carefully used it to rearrange their pattern into a rough circle. Mr Tracy asked if it shouldn't be a square, but my boy only shook his head and continued the shaping.

Pepsi made most of the decisions for us now. At times I found it almost impossible to believe he was a child, much less my own. How shocked his father, Peter Graf, would have been to see all this! I wondered why *he* had never appeared in Rondua, but then it struck me that I had made the ultimate decision to abort Pepsi. Peter was only a small-spirited, arrogant man who'd considered abortion another form of birth control. I had been the one to climb on to that hospital table and say, 'Yes, I'm ready now.' I even remembered using those exact words.

Curiously, however, I still didn't believe abortion was wrong for other women. Our actions and responsibilities are our own: what later returns to either haunt or applaud us is neither possible to predict nor always completely understandable.

I approached the Laughing Hat boat at the same time as Pepsi climbed in. It was silent now; only the upside-down face was still smiling broadly. Inside it were several wooden boxes full of food and plastic bottles of what I took to be drinking water.

Pepsi was moving things around inside. There were two bench seats opposite each other. Although everything was in beautiful condition, with the wood polished to a shine, it looked like the inside of any row-boat you would take out for half an hour on Sunday on Central Park Lake. Only here the Sea of Brynn stretched to the horizon and I knew we would be out on it for at least one night, if not longer.

'There's the sail, Mom, but we can catch the current and use it for a while. It'll take us out even if we don't put the sail up.'

'How do you know this stuff, Peps?'

He shrugged and smiled—don't bother me, Mom, I know—all there on his face.

'Mr Tracy, will you be here when we get back?'

'If you find the Bone, yes.'

Far behind us in the distance, sounds of muted thunder broke the quiet. We all turned from the sea and saw smudges of ugly dark smoke rising thick and fast over the land we had so recently crossed.

'The cats are dead now,' Martio said and looked at Mr Tracy. 'Cats, perfect fossils and freshwater wells.' The camel knelt slowly down into a sitting position on his knees.

Mr Tracy kept looking at the smoke. 'Cats, new music and steam on glass. They're all gone. Other things too. Pepsi, you've got to hurry.'

We pushed the boat to the edge of the water, which had begun to roll and churn moodily. From shore the animals watched as we bounced and slipped our way out on to the grumbling sea. As soon as the brown sail went up, it snapped once and filled completely. Pepsi held the tiller and steered with the confidence of an old salt. He had so many new tricks up his sleeve: talent, insight, magic. What had been the meaning of rearranging the rabbit star? How had he known the proper sorcery to make Felina's body disappear? What map had he studied to show him the direction to go on the sea?

'Pepsi, what would have happened if you had been born in my world?'

'Mae would have been my sister, Mom.' He wouldn't look at me.

'Yes, I know that, but what else? Do you know what your life would have been?' He shook his head and watched the sea. 'Look at me, Pepsi. Do you hate me?'

'You're my Mom, why would I hate you? You came here to help me. You're my best friend! Hey look, way over there, do you see that island? It's called Ais. You should see what's on there!'

I looked at Ais Island and wondered what it was, what it 'meant'. Was it someone else's Rondua, or only another blip of land in a pink ocean, where rocks cried or clouds stood quiet guard over iron cattle with human voices.

Rondua. You could change things here: save your child from the City of the Dead. But what happened after that, if it happened at all? And how could I change anything when I knew so goddamned little, felt so stupid and weak every time I encountered something new or different?

'Mom, I think we're there! Yeah, we're there already. Boy, we made it! Look down, Mom. Look down there through the water. You can see everything!'

The day had slowly ended and the sun, in no hurry, was slipping over the edge of earth. Because we had been talking, I hadn't really noticed that the colour of the sea had changed from its original all-pink to a combination of gold, pure plum and some fiery orange mixed in too—the colours of motor oil on top of a puddle of water.

At first this sharp colour change was more than enough to startle me, but then I did what Pepsi said: stared down through the water.

124

My God, there was *land* down there! Green and beige and hard blue land. The colours you see from an aeroplane window in the middle of your journey. But that blue was water and only then did I realize the Sea of Brynn wasn't a sea at all, but the sky. We sat in our laughing hat/boat in the *sky,* floating softly across a sunset. Instead of watching it from the ground, we were smack-dab in the centre of it—sailing across a sky of changing twilight colours, countless miles above . . . the Earth? I had no idea at all.

I tried to keep my voice as calm as I could. 'Pepsi, where are we?'

'We have to go really fast now, Mom. You'd better sit down.'

A wind redolent of oranges and cloves drove us steadily forward across the darkening sea/sky. Fish leapt around us and I knew their names before they called them out to us: Mudrake, Cornsweat, Yasmuda. They were followed by red fish that, when they broke the surface, became huge wolves. I remembered Felina's stories about the evolution of her ancestors and I missed her even more when I saw those wolves in wet flight. A school of pure white dolphins swam next to us for more than an hour, our funny boat moving easily alongside them. Their leader was named Ulla and before they disappeared, she lifted us on to her ivory back and sped us forward for miles.

I remember all of this. It is true and it will always be true for me. If I close my eyes this minute I can still smell that pink sea, the oranges and cloves.

Many hours later, when the eclipse came, the wind stopped completely and the stars disappeared as one. We slowed for some time, then bumped hard into something which stopped our forward movement completely: a small rock island.

'Ah ha! My sailors have arrived. Good, good! Welcome, visitors, you're just about on time. Wait a minute and I'll get us some light. Come on up on land.'

The slick-slop of water on the sides of the boat was cut by the *swish* of a match. That was followed by the slow eerie hiss and glow of a propane gas-lamp coming to life.

'Cullen, you're the vegetarian, so I made you a couple of cheese and tomato sandwiches. Is that okay? And for Pepsi, there's peanut butter and jelly. Real American peanut butter too! Let's eat first and then we can talk. I've been waiting in the dark for you two for hours.'

125

The man handed us sandwiches tightly wrapped in aluminium foil.

'Pepsi and I already know each other, Cullen. But I'm sure you've forgotten me. It's been such a long time since we last met. My name is DeFazio.'

He was dressed in boating shoes, blue jeans and a white sweatshirt. About fifty, he had a crew-cut and the face of a tired commuter riding in the bar car at the end of the day: nondescript, middle-management, owner of a station wagon with fake wood sides, a mortgaged house, lots of stress.

'How very right you are, Cullen! I'm one of a million men in a grey flannel suit. Powerless, but I manage to smile a lot in between drinks. I think it's only fair to tell you before we go on that I can read your mind. Don't be frightened, though—it's unimportant. Would you like another sandwich, either of you? No? Okay, then maybe it's best if we begin. I have the fourth Bone. In fact, it's right here. Wait a minute.'

He reached into a white canvas bag and brought out something that looked like a dark baseball.

'It's strange-looking, isn't it?' He shrugged and rolled it in his hand. 'It's yours if you want it. Just stick it in your pocket and off you go.

'Hey, don't look so surprised! Were you two expecting a big fire-breathing dragon? Not at all, that's not necessary. Your trip out here in that ridiculous boat was enough adventure for one day, no?'

Our expressions must have blared distrust because he smiled and shook his head.

'You don't believe me? Really, I am *not* going to do anything to you. It's not what you think. The fourth Bone is yours, free and clear. It's the only one you don't have to fight for. Don't you remember *anything*, Cullen? That's one of the great tricks of the game. Some people have got so scared thinking what would happen to them if they were to come out here, they just back off and run away.

'Anyway, look you've already seen what things are like now. Jack Chili may be in power, but the whole scene back there on land is so chaotic and scattered that it really doesn't matter who's in charge, does it? On the one hand, you have your Sizzling Thumb, Heeg, Solaris and good old mighty Chili himself. You haven't met him yet, have you? Plenty of time for that! And there are others too, believe

126

it or not—animal, vegetable *and* mineral! All of them want to rule. All of them want power. But you know what? Every one of them is just hopeful and silly. Hopeful and silly—perfect adjectives for this hopeless place. The Land of Laughs, if you ask me. Only it so happens, they're the wrong kind of laughs.

'You know the kind—funny but not so funny? The talentless person who insists on singing at the talent show? Or how about the midget walking down the street with a big cigar in his mouth? You know the kind of laugh I'm talking about. Pathetic!' DeFazio shook his head and took a bite of his sandwich. 'I'm not being completely fair. Rondua is a wonderful place; you've seen enough of it to know that. Sometimes I get off this damned island and go back for a quick look. Didn't you love the Caves of Lem? They're the most beautiful things. Even your friend Gregston was impressed. I'm sorry; I'm rambling, aren't I? Here is what you want to know: I'm DeFazio, caretaker (among other things) of the fourth Bone of the Moon. You can have it right here and now. Get in and drive it away—no money down, folks. But don't think I'm doing you a favour. Giving it to you without a warning is the meanest thing I could do.

'Look, if you *do* take it and go back, you'll meet up sooner or later with Jack Chili. You'll have to fight him for the fifth Bone. I can't tell you any more than that, but it will take an impossible amount of courage to go up against him. But let me finish the scenario anyway so that you have the full picture. The fifth Bone completes the quest. Get it, and you become the ruler of Rondua. Chili is out and you're in.

'But *that's* the biggest joke of all, Pepsi. Believe me! Because ruling doesn't mean you rule—it means you *try* to rule! You assemble all of these hopeful, silly, *mean* beings back there. Get them under one roof and tell them what's best for them. And you will be right, because winning the Bones gives you that kind of wisdom, I won't deny you that. But do you think they'll care for a minute? Not on your life! They'll listen to you because they'll respect your achievement. That's something they'd never even dream of accomplishing. But that's superfluous, because in the end they'll eye each other malevolently and hate everyone around them who owns what they don't. Oh, of course they'll listen politely to you. But then they'll run back home and start massing their absurd little armies for yet another silly, hopeless battle.'

He got up and walked away from our small circle of lamplight.

His footsteps in the dark were very loud and he spoke again from a few feet away.

'Do you know what? History teaches us that the only great rulers are dead ones: the ones we look at in museums and history books and say, "Oh, how right he was! Why didn't any of those stupid people back then listen to him! Why would anyone want to assassinate that great mind?"

'Okay, Pepsi, let's say for a minute that you get exactly what you want: you become ruler of Rondua. *Nothing* will change! Take my word for it! Absolutely nothing. Sure, you'll have the power to control them, but you can take it for granted they'll hate you, *despise* you even, for holding all that power over them. And once your back is turned, they'll do what they like best of all—they'll pull out their swords or talons or fire and stick them into the nearest enemy. Listen to me! Wise men, even great men, never put a stop to hatred and enemies. They just pull them apart for a little while. That's why Jack Chili has been so successful in his reign—he doesn't *have* to lift a finger to cause trouble. Man causes his own trouble. Trouble is the only perpetual motion machine there is!'

Pepsi's small voice off to my right made me blink hard. 'I don't like you, Mr DeFazio.'

A sad chuckle. 'I don't like myself, little king. Your son dislikes me, Cullen, not because of what I have been saying but because I took him to Ophir Zik when he first . . . arrived here. I could excuse myself by saying that's only part of my assigned job here in Rondua, but I won't do that because it's a flimsy excuse. The truth is, like so many others in this universe I've grown completely indifferent . . . even to things like taking children to the City of the Dead. At the same time, I've also become a great supporter of the status quo, if you know what I mean. I believe in keeping things on an even keel and hope that lightning strikes someone else when it begins to fall. I don't question, don't challenge, don't debate. I do exactly what I'm told and then it's time to go home for a drink.

'In the meantime, I have come to the conclusion that life has a very bad case of acne which it has no desire to lose, because that would mean it couldn't look in the mirror fifty times a day and feel so sorry for itself.'

'That's a very clever, very shitty philosophy, Mr DeFazio.'

Pepsi giggled and I smiled, liking both his giggle and what I'd said.

'Cullen, people like you love the view from up there on your high horses, don't you? The glory of human virtue! All Hail! I'll do this and one day they'll give me a statue in the park! Here, take the Bone!' He had been tossing it back and forth from hand to hand for several minutes; putting it down on the ground, he rolled it across the sand towards Pepsi.

'Can we go now?'

'Of course! Why would I stop you? Do you think *I* want to fight Jack Chili? There are two problems with being a statue in the park, Cullen. First, you have to be dead. Second, once you're there, the birds shit all over you. I leave those pleasures to you. The fourth Bone is yours. You've been warned. Good luck with Jack Chili!'

'Our friends, Mom! There they are!'

Mr Tracy and Martio stood in the surf, their paws raised high in the air in greeting. What a welcome sight! The uneventful trip back, although hurried along by another fast wind, was crowded for me with worries about our future.

DeFazio said no more after giving Pepsi the Bone. Hunched by the fire, his face said everything I didn't want to know—bad things were ahead, pain as common as a breeze, thirty flavours of fear. I'd hated nothing in Rondua until him; his complacent fatalism scared me more than any of the growling monsters and moving nightmares we had encountered along our way. I had known a Mr DeFazio in college, and then a few of them after I'd graduated. To people like them, creativity, excitement and joy were all cute little flukes of nature, as doomed and impossible as the dodo bird. And look what happened to *that* animal, they liked to observe in between yawns, sighs and weary shrugs. They were summed up by a line I'd read in a French poem somewhere: 'The flesh is sad, alas, and I've read all the books.' The way they saw it, you lived and died and along the way you learned not to give a damn, because it all ends up dead and stinking so what's the use?

The ominous part was that they were right much of the time and only had to point in a number of directions to prove it.

But I had been blessed or lucky enough to know that great things did exist and were constantly available, only you had to wrestle them away from life because it held these treasures close to its chest and gave them up only after you had proved yourself a worthy opponent.

Not that I had had to fight for many of the prizes that were mine, but being one of the lucky ones had only made me more aware of how important it was to appreciate them every minute. And how important it was to go to the wall protecting them when bad came around, looking for trouble.

Pepsi jumped out of the boat and splashed up the shore, where he hugged each animal and told them in a rush about our night on the sea and run-in with Mr DeFazio. I joined them and waited until he was finished before speaking.

'Who *is* Jack Chili, Mr Tracy?'

Pepsi was hugging Martio for the tenth time and seemed very much the little boy again. The camel was smiling happily and watching us.

'He's a man with wings. He's a bird with fins. I can't tell you what you'll see when you see him, Cullen, because he's different for everyone. When I was young and saw him for the first time, he was a book with the same word on every page.'

'Why is he called Jack Chili?'

'That's only one of his names. What's interesting is, you'll have your own name for him when you see him.'

'What does he do? Why is everyone afraid of him?'

'They're afraid of him because he hates everything that isn't his. He lives in a beautiful valley and causes trouble everywhere. You don't remember him at all, Cullen?'

'No, nothing.'

'Maybe that's better. Would you like to go to sleep now? We can take our time; you two must be exhausted.'

All four of us curled up together on the damp beach, Pepsi and I sandwiched in on either side by the animals. I lay against Martio's warm stomach and watched the pure pearl of the morning sky above us. I felt sleepy, but wanted to stay awake a little longer so I could savour the calmness of the moment and the giant softness of my animal bed. I tried to match my breathing with Martio's, but his was so long and slow that I quickly fell out of rhythm. There were still so many questions to ask, but they could wait until later when our minds weren't so completely tired and full of recent memories. When I slept, I dreamt of a giant black fountain-pen writing words across the sky: words that made no sense, but were very beautiful nonetheless.

When we awoke, the sea was completely gone. Even Pepsi was

surprised by its disappearance. In its place was an immense meadow full of wild flowers and crazy-coloured butterflies. It was very warm and sunny.

A picnic was laid out nearby and one look at what was there told me how hungry I was. The animals were nowhere around, but for the moment eating was more important than their whereabouts. Both Pepsi and I pounced on the food and ate everything up.

A sign of our having grown accustomed to the wonders of Rondua was the fact that neither of us bothered to say anything about the transformation of the Sea of Brynn into a field of brilliantly-coloured flowers. It was just different now and there was no reason to expect an explanation.

In a much smaller way, it reminded me of how I had finally grown used to Europe's ways after having lived there for a year. People washed the steps of their houses in Europe. You had to buy matches for your cigarettes, and it was against the law to walk your dog during the day in Russia. Where did these things come from? Who knows? It all just *was* and you got used to it.

Granted, in Rondua everything was bigger and wilder, but it really wasn't that different.

We sat for an hour feeling warm and comfortably fat. Expecting the animals to return at any time, we didn't think anything had happened until the first negnug appeared. They moved so quietly through the high soft grass that neither of us knew they were there until one ran under Pepsi's bent knee.

'Come immediately! Come immediately or it will be too late!'

As black as coal and with fur as smooth as a house cat's, the little animal looked like a miniature ant-eater with a nose like a funnel and two bright raisin-small eyes.

But what shocked me most was that I *remembered* them! As a girl, I had drawn pictures of negnugs and had even given them their name after careful, seven-year-old consideration. I drew pictures of them all the time—negnugs driving cars, in bed with plaid pillows and foot-warmers, riding on a ferris wheel. My mother saved these drawings because she thought they were so cute and imaginative. She gave me some of them when I was in college; I even remembered in what drawer of the desk I kept them at home.

'Don't think about that! Think about now, Cullen. Come immediately!'

Through the mental fog of almost twenty years, I recognized the

131

high, silly, urgent voice I had originally imagined a negnug would have.

A second one appeared at its side and then a third. They were very upset about something and all three began jumping up and down when neither Pepsi nor I moved.

Pepsi was smiling. 'What are they saying, Mom? Do you understand them?'

Shock number two! *I* could understand them, but he couldn't. He was clearly delighted by their presence, but had no idea of what they were talking about.

'Come! Come! It's Mr Tracy. He's hurt! He might die! Hurry up!'

We were running with them, but it was plain the negnugs were capable of going ten times faster although they were holding back their speed for our sake. Pepsi and I had started out holding hands and running together, but soon he broke the clasp and sprinted ahead.

'I must go faster, Mom! You catch up!'

After ten minutes, the heavy meal we'd just eaten began to weigh me down. Then a sharp, painful stitch rose up in my side and I slowed to a worried jog, but even that was hard to do. Luckily it was only a few minutes more before I saw the big black body lying on its side, so out of place in that pretty field of flowers.

The air smelled of lilacs, although I had never seen lilacs in Rondua. Pepsi was down on his knees next to Mr Tracy, chanting something I had never heard before. I saw that one of the dog's hind legs was gone, although the ragged stump looked as if it had already been cleanly closed and cauterized.

Mr Tracy's eye was open, but was as empty of life as I'd ever seen. The whole picture was dreadful and alarming, but a moment later I remembered something from deep in my past that saved everything.

Rushing forward, I shoved Pepsi aside and took his place. Then I reached into the boy's bag and took out the fourth Bone of the Moon, Slee.

'Get his mouth open! I've got to put this one in there.'

Pepsi and I pulled the dog's cold jaws apart and finally wide enough to shove the fourth Bone in. There was a loud clacking sound when we let go and the mouth snapped shut again. That was an awful sound: a dead sound.

The negnugs squealed and ran around as if they'd gone mad. I took my hands away and waited; it was one of the only times I had ever known exactly what to do in Rondua.

Some time passed and then Mr Tracy blinked slowly. Something in him returned from very far away.

I felt as if I were suddenly lighter. I knew what had happened— my last memory of magic was gone now. I'd carried it with me since returning to Rondua without knowing it.

But now a tremendous wave of memory crashed over me, telling me everything I had forgotten for so long. When I was a child in Rondua, pursuing the fifth Bone, I had used Slee wrongly. As a result, all of the creatures who had accompanied me on that long and dangerous trip died unnecessarily. At the last second I had panicked and saved myself without thought for the others. I had used the magic of one of the Bones thoughtlessly, selfishly . . .

Fear's greatest weapon is its ability to blind one to anything. In its presence, we forget there are others to consider, things to save besides ourselves. That was my great irreparable mistake the first time I had been in Rondua. It was that panic and that selfishness that had kept me from winning the fifth Bone of the Moon.

When he spoke, Mr Tracy's words came out tiredly and with the greatest difficulty. 'I was so wrong. I trusted him . . . completely!' His eye stared straight at me, full of sad wonder.

'Who? What are you talking about, Mr Tracy?'

Pepsi spoke from behind me. 'Martio. Martio is Jack Chili, Mom. He was fooling us the whole time. Now he knows everything.'

4

Dear Mrs James,

Dr Lavery keeps asking me why I chose an axe to hurt my mother and sister with. He said it might help me to understand what I'd done better if I think about just that part of it for a while. He also said if I couldn't tell him directly, then I should try to tell you in one of my letters, so I will do that.

Death is really interesting to me. I think about it a lot and I have read many books on the subject. I don't know if there is a heaven or a hell, but I *do* think we go someplace special after it's all over.

I read this book, *Shogun,* all about Japan and its samurai warriors. I think those men had it all figured out. The way they saw it, if you lived the right kind of life—full of courage and boldness—then dying honourably was the only thing that mattered. There were men in that book who actually *asked* to be able to die for their leader. If they were granted permission by the leader (and not all of them were, believe me!), then they thought they were very lucky and went right out and killed themselves. My mother and sister were both very good women and I felt that if they died at that time in their lives, then they would most assuredly be allowed to go wherever it is good people go after they're dead. Granted, my sister played her stereo much too loud and my mother wasn't always the kindest person on earth to me, but those things were not important in the long run. They were good women—both of them— who had reached a special level where, if they died just when they did, they'd be allowed to move right on. I kept hoping before I took action that they would die on an aeroplane they took to my uncle's house in Florida, but it didn't happen unfortunately. They survived the trip, so it was up to me to see that they made it safely through to the other side— which is exactly what I did.

Why did I use that axe? I don't know. Maybe because my father kept it around from the time when we had a house out in the country. Do you know the town of Dobbs Ferry, New York? That's where it was. Those years out there were the best I ever had in my life. My sister and I were young and we liked each other very much.

I don't know why . . . Oh, this is stupid, isn't it? I started out trying to explain to you about the axe and now where am I? Stupid. Really stupid! Dr Lavery asks me all the time if I'm sorry I did it. Sure, I'm sorry, but on the other hand I very seriously feel that they died at just the right time—just like those lucky samurai warriors in *Shogun*. That's why I did them a kind of special favour. To me, that takes away a lot of the wrong.

Did this letter bore you?

Yours very sincerely,
Alvin Williams

'Dr Lavery?'

'Yes, Mrs James?'

'Dr Lavery, did you see the last letter Alvin Williams wrote to me?'

'Yes, I did. I'm sorry I didn't get to you before it did. I had it down on my calendar to call; it was wrong of me not to do it.'

'But why didn't you intercept it, Doctor? Why did you let it go through?'

'Because Alvin is very protective of his correspondence with you, Mrs James. He reads me all of your letters and is always very worried if you don't answer his questions.'

'Well, I'm very sorry, Doctor, but I don't want to do this any more. This last letter scared the hell out of me and I don't want that to happen again. I've been shaking all morning. Would you please tell him to stop writing to me? Because even if he keeps it up, I'm not going to write back to him. I don't ever want to see a letter like that again.'

'I fully understand, Mrs James. I'll tell Alvin this afternoon.'

There was a pause and then I asked the inevitable: 'What will it do to him if I stop writing, Doctor?'

'Naturally it will upset him. Mrs James; you're one of his only links to the outside world now. If that is suddenly broken, he'll be scared and angry. That's understandable. He won't know what he's done wrong, yet he's being punished for it by someone he cares so much about.'

'Oh great! You make me feel guilty.'

'Guilt is relative, Mrs James. I understand why you're upset, but there's really no reason to feel guilty. We have a variety of therapies available to us that we can use in cases like Alvin's. The correspondence with you was simply one part of one of them.'

'What do you mean?'

'We've been trying to reconnect him with the real world, Mrs James. We give him books to read, encourage him to plan for a future, let him have an outside friend he can write to in as normal a way as possible. Now, if that plan worked and he responded, first we would try to bring him back to our world, as it were. Once there, we'd hopefully be able to show him what he'd done wrong on a real-life scale. Right now, the great problem we're having with Alvin is that he honestly doesn't yet understand the enormity of his act. If we were successful, then we would begin to try reintegrating him into the system he so violently broke out of through his . . . aggressive acts.'

I bit the inside of my lips while he spoke.

'All of it makes sense, Doctor, and obviously you know best about these things, but this letter scared the hell out of me, you know? All of his letters do. Each time one arrives and I realize who it's from, it sets me back at least a couple of days. It makes me jumpy and . . . grumpy . . . Do you know what I mean? Do you understand?'

'I understand completely, Mrs James. You have every right to ask that they stop.'

'Well, is he getting any better? Have you seen any signs of progress?'

'That's another relative term. Off the record, he's still very much the same disturbed young man he was when he came in, but we're certainly working on it.'

'Doctor, am I being a big rat by doing this?'

Luckily he laughed, which made me feel a little better. 'Absolutely not! In fact, your wanting to stop the correspondence might be an effective device for us. Alvin will certainly be upset and he'll want to know your reasons for doing it. But perhaps with some hedging here and there, what I tell him will make him better understand the fact that if he really *does* want to become a member of

136

society again, he'll have to come to grips with the fact that most people are made very nervous when they come into contact with someone who's done what he has. Yes, I think it might be the right time to talk with him about this. Your act will be just the right thing to trigger the discussion. You've given me another angle, Mrs James. I hadn't thought of using it before, but it makes perfect sense to me now.'

'This may be a dumb question, Doctor, but what *is* going to happen to him?'

'It's not a dumb question at all. Sooner or later he will realize what he has done and why he did it. Or else he'll stay in the Institute for the rest of his life, confused and resentful of the fact that we're holding him here against his will. It could go either way.'

'He *really* doesn't understand what he's done?'

'From all indications so far? No. He's recently been going through a phase that is very common for patients like Alvin: he's convinced he's some kind of god! He feels he took those lives because they belonged to him in the first place. Do you remember his references to the novel *Shogun*? Well, Alvin envisions himself as some kind of supreme shogun these days. He sees himself as the most powerful, most fearsome, wisest leader around. That's why he liked that book so much: he turned its plot and ideas around this way and that, and ended up making them fit his own patterns. He's extremely good at doing that. Do you know what he's been doing the last couple of days? Studying Japanese!

'Not long ago, you'll remember, he wanted to be a veterinarian. When you think about it, it's very much the same thing. The only difference is, a vet controls life and death in animals. God, *or a* Japanese shogun, controls those things in human beings.'

I ended my pen-pal days with Alvin Williams, but that didn't stop me from thinking about him. At funny times of the day, pictures and questions would run across my mind; what kind of clothes did he wear in the Institute? What did *he* dream about at night? Did he listen to music? Did he ever finish reading *Shogun*?

Since I hadn't seen him for so long, his plain unmemorable face and ways slipped quickly out of my memory's clear focus. But I remembered the way he described those storm clouds that day—as if they were having a fist-fight. I remembered his dirty eye-glasses and the way he walked slowly down the stairs with Loopy, their little old dog who couldn't move too fast. I don't know how to say this, but there was a part of me that wished Alvin well, despite what I had done to push him away from my life.

'Hello, Cullen? This is Weber.'

'Weber. How *are* you?'

'Fine! Listen, I'm on my way to California; I'm at the airport right now. I've been trying to get you for a couple of days. Cullen, I've got to tell you—the dreams? The Rondua dreams? They're better. You can't believe what a change there's been. Ever since we went out, they've become the most amazing things. It's beautiful!'

'What do you mean, Weber? Are you still having dreams there? Are you still having those nightmares?'

'Not at all. Hey, I look *forward* to going to sleep at night! Yeah, I'm still in Rondua, but it's become . . . something entirely different. There's no dark stuff any more, only wonders. Only beautiful, amazing things. I love it. It's like the old days, when we used to do drugs? But the good drugs, the pure ones that flew you right off the earth? I can't tell you how many new ideas it's given me for my new movie. It's all a mishmash right now, but I know it's going to be incredible when I get everything all sorted out. What was that word you used? The magic one?'

'Koukounaries?'

'That's it. Koukounaries. Well, it worked. I can't tell you. I've got to go! I'll be back in a couple of weeks. Can we go out to lunch and talk about it? Oh Christ, they're closing my gate. I'll call you! Cullen, hey, thanks a lot! God, I've got to tell you everything. Bye!'

On my birthday, my friend Danny James did something so crazy and lovely that I was speechless for almost five minutes.

We had arranged for Eliot to babysit with Mae while we went out for dinner. Danny hadn't given me a present, but our financial situation was such that I took it for granted the dinner alone would send our cheque-book screaming.

It was a Friday night and, in general, New York was jumpy and electric and ready for its weekend. Even the weirdos and walking dead on street corners looked less hopeless and more sane than usual.

Danny knew about Alvin Williams' last letter and my conversation with Dr Lavery. As a result, he did all he could to cheer me up and make me laugh. He did a good job, too. Danny was never flashy funny; he didn't tell many jokes or make cute faces or speak in little Mr Elf-y voices, but he could still crack me up whenever he wanted. If nothing else, all he had to do was tell a James family story and that did it. For some reason, crazy things happened to the James family all the time. On the night of my birthday, I heard the tale of Uncle Gene. Uncle Gene James had played professional baseball in South America for a few years, and once had gone to bat against none other than Fidel Castro when Gene's team was in Cuba. Apparently, Castro is a big baseball buff and loves nothing more than to get out on the field and throw a few. This time out, Gene was lead-off hitter against the famous hurler. Castro, wearing his army uniform, threw exactly one curveball which hit Gene right on the head. He recovered, but wild pitches are *not* good public relations for the leader of a country. After the game, when Gene was in the locker room holding an ice-pack against his skull, two gorillas in military uniform came up and said if he ever let out about the beanball, he'd be turned into black bean soup.

'Those fuckin' Commies!' This came from the cab-driver who had been eavesdropping on Danny's story the whole time. His face in the rear-view mirror looked just as if it had been bitten by a wasp right in the middle.

I took Danny's hand and squeezed my choked laughter through it.

'Even when you're just playin' baseball, they try to get you!'

Danny winked at me, then asked the driver where he'd got his swell cap.

'Not in no Russia, I'll tell you *that*, Ace!'

Dinner was at a place in Chelsea which Eliot had recommended as having some of the best food in town. It lived up to his word and we ate ourselves into proud stupors.

After dinner, Danny reached into his pocket and pulled out a thick envelope. 'Do you want to guess, or should I show you?'

'Yippee! Show me, Dan! I hate guessing.'

Opening the envelope, he pulled out passports and two bright red and green aeroplane tickets.

'In exactly three hours, birthday girl, you and I are going to get on the midnight flight to Milano, Italy. We're there until Monday, and we're staying in the Brera at the Solferino. What do you think of that, Colon?'

'I think I like it a lot, Captain, but what about our daughter?'

'She's already with your parents—it's all been arranged. Eliot took her over right after we left the house. That's why they didn't all come out to dinner with us.'

'We can't afford this, can we, Danny?'

'Nope. Oh, maybe one-ninth of it. Do you want dessert? I saw a great-looking chocolate cake when we came in.'

Despite a sleepless, *multo agitato* ride over the ocean, we arrived on Saturday afternoon in Milan wide-awake and crazy to get out and get started in Italy again. On the short trip in from the airport, we tried to decide what to do first: walk, or shop, or visit our beloved 'Marchesi' for cappuccino and *dolce.* We agreed right off (and shook on it to make it binding) that there would be no rules that weekend. You could do or eat or have seconds on whatever you wanted, and no one was allowed to raise an eyebrow in disapproval.

The first part of that day was the most relaxing time I had had in a long while. Mae, Weber, Alvin Williams . . . not to mention the ever-frisky Rondua at night had filled my life to the top of its cup constantly. That was all fine, but there weren't many moments for calm thought and/or reflection amidst that 3-D circus of mine.

I didn't know how much I'd missed or needed that relaxation until I was sitting alone in a café in the great Galleria, reading a magazine and having a glass of chilled fresh orange juice. Danny was off wandering the Via della Spiga, but I had decided it was just about time to sit back and take it easy for a while. My body yearned to feel heavy and content, sitting like a happy log at an exquisite Italian café, watching the rest of the world wander by.

After a good hour, I noticed something I had completely forgotten about. European women are so completely different from Americans. There seems to be so much pride attached to *being* different from men over there—and not just in Italy either—to being special because you are, thank God, a woman.

On the other hand many American women, whether they're twenty or forty, seem so raw and graceless in comparison. In general, they move badly, talk like 'good old boys', chew gum with their mouths open, wear misshapen clothes . . . And even though they wear a lot of make-up I always have the impression the majority of them would like nothing more than to be 'one of the guys'.

As a result, when we lived in Europe (and now again after only an

140

hour in the café, watching), I felt like ET's rural cousin when I held myself up to the women around me.

There aren't many beggars in Milan, but the ones who do work the streets are certainly a colourful bunch. Almost always women, they deck themselves out in gypsy kerchiefs and ragged dresses that fall to the tops of their bare feet. They inevitably carry an infant at a dangerous angle on one arm and come up to you with palm extended, looking as if they're about to cry.

I didn't notice the one who approached me until she was almost rubbing my shoulder. Looking up, a little dazed and still far away in my thoughts, I didn't register the change on her face until she leapt back and spoke to me.

'Strega!'

Strega is the popular Italian drink. It is also the word for witch.

Shocked by both the word and her tone of voice, I looked from her to the baby in her arms. It was Mae.

'Mae! My baby!'

I got up so quickly that I knocked my chair over and a waiter standing nearby yelled at the woman to get out.

'She has my baby!'

I said it in English, but the waiter understood and grabbed the woman by the arm.

'Strega! Maligna!'

What followed would have been funny if it hadn't been so awful. The child came alive and started crying and when I saw its face I realized it wasn't Mae at all. But that recognition didn't make me feel any better because something just as bad dawned on me: the woman's face was familiar.

My dream of months before: women sweeping the floor with fiery scarves, threatening my daughter if I continued to help Pepsi in Rondua. This woman was one of them, I was sure of that.

She pulled away from the waiter and ran across the floor of the Galleria, looking at me over her shoulder as she ran. I didn't want her to come back, but unconsciously I put up my hand in her direction.

No purple light spun out of my hand in a hard arc as it had with Weber Gregston, but a hundred feet across the way the woman lifted off the ground and fell in a screaming heap. Had I done it, or had she simply fallen?

It would have ended there if she hadn't continued to yell at me,

141

but I no longer knew what she was saying. Her words had become all short spits and crazy, whirling gestures. Thank God, the child was okay!

The commotion that followed was confusing and ugly; it lasted about twenty minutes. Besides the woman and me, it involved two policemen, the waiter and a number of 'eyewitnesses'.

The police wanted to know if that *was* my child—had the woman stolen anything from me, did I want to press charges? They didn't ask her one thing, although she continued to yell until one of them threatened to take her to jail unless she shut up.

When it was over, they told her to get out of there. Touching their hats to me, they gave me one last suspicious look and then followed her out to make sure she left. The poor waiter, who was completely baffled by then, kindly asked if I wanted another *spremuta*. It was obvious though that he wanted me out of there too and the whole thing forgotten. I said no and gave him ten thousand lira for his trouble.

I immediately went to a post office and—without thinking—called my parents in New York to see if Mae was okay. They thought it was very cute that I was so concerned, but it *was* the middle of the night there and they hoped the ringing hadn't wakened her. My mother reminded me to bring home a big piece of Parmesan cheese and told me not to waste my time in Italy worrying. I felt very foolish, but greatly reassured.

When I met up with Danny again an hour later, he told me he had called a bunch of our friends and arranged for all of us to have dinner together later. We spent the rest of the day wandering around and that was nice, but the scene earlier had slapped me hard in the face and left it stinging and bright red.

Luckily, dinner was a rowdy three hours that did a great deal towards making things better. Familiar stories, heavenly food and funny, entertaining people reminded me once again of how first-rate living in Italy had been for us.

Everyone wanted to see pictures of Mae and I gladly obliged. Two of them decided after seeing the snaps that she must marry their sons in a few years and have Italian *bambini*. I didn't dare ask how she was to manage two husbands at the same time!

We ate and talked and it seemed as if someone was always gesturing wildly or else refilling everyone's glass with red wine. Danny sat directly across from me, wedged between two old basketball team-mates; he looked very happy. Once in a while he would look over to make sure I was getting along all right. Good tears came to my eyes more than once that evening, and not only when they brought out a birthday cake. There were no candles, but Lorenzo remedied that by taking one from the table and jamming it into the middle of the cake, much to the waiter's dismay.

'Make a weesh, Cullen!'

'Yes, wish that we win some more games next year!'

'Hey, *fungione*, it's her birthday today, not yours!'

I closed my eyes and wished the fifth Bone of the Moon for Pepsi. I certainly had everything I wanted.

At the hotel afterwards, we decided to take a bath together. Halfway through, we made slow, funny love right there in the tub. We hadn't done that in a long time and I thought it was perfect and hilarious. Danny asked what was so funny and the only thing I could answer was, 'Our knees, our knees!' which didn't clarify much.

The nice thing about sex is that you can use it for so many different things: to get hot, to cement a bond or—in the case of that moment for us—to be little kids again together, having a great sexy time.

When we'd untangled ourselves from the love tub, Danny dried off fast and disappeared into the bedroom in a suspicious hurry.

'What are you doing?'

'You'll see.'

I looked at my reflection in the mirror and frowned. 'Danny . . .'

'Be quiet and just come in here when you're ready.'

I wrapped a towel around me and marched in . . .

When I came to Europe and joined Danny in Greece, one day I found on a beach the most beautiful piece of bottle glass I'd ever seen. Bottle glass? It's glass that has been in the ocean so long that, broken or not at one time, all of its corners have since become rounded and smooth. What's even better if you've come across a special piece, is that it has the most gentle, washed-out, unearthly colour imaginable. I have seen it the strange grey-blue of cigarette smoke as it disappears in the air, or the fragile pink of a baby's tongue. Of course it all depends on what colour the glass was originally and how long it has been washing around under water. Many people collect it with a strange passion and I can understand that, because good bottle glass is like nothing you've ever seen before. Enchantingly, I found my piece on one of the first days in Europe and naturally I took that as a great omen. I treasured it for many reasons, but particularly because it meant so many things all at once. Every time I looked at it on my dresser—it was about the size of a fifty-cent piece—it *was* 1. Danny James; 2. the first days in Greece; 3. Europe; 4. Love; 5. My first great courage . . . all of it there in a small mysterious piece of glass.

This night in Milan it was sitting on top of one of the pillows. Danny had taken it to a jeweller and had a small hole drilled at the top, so that he could thread it on the thin gold chain that he'd bought. I could wear the whole beautiful thing as a necklace. I'd often mentioned wanting to do just that, if and when we ever came into a little extra loot.

It was a complete Danny James gift—loving, thoughtful, intimate. I went over and gave him a bear-hug.

'You're such a big . . . treasure. You know that, Danny? Thank you very much.'

'You're welcome. I think you're losing your towel there.'

I pulled him down on to the bed and at half-speed, as sexily as I could, put his necklace on, watching him closely the whole time. My body felt charged with electricity, which made my skin hot and tight and tingly. We were both ready again, but it had to be slow now. Not funny or friendly-slow as it had been before in the bath-tub. Now it would be thick-slow; blood pounding in your head, slow. Don't touch yet—not yet. Wait and look, look until you can't stand it any more, then wait more.

He understood. We had done it this way before, but because it was Milan and my birthday, and as much magic in the air as we'd ever have between us, we waited even longer. Danny's only move was to put one hot finger under the golden necklace and jiggle it lightly. I felt it all across my breasts. We were still looking straight into each other's eyes.

'Happy birthday, my Cullen.'

Later, dripping and exhausted, I fell right to sleep. I dreamt we visited the grave of our daughter.

I figured we missed the call by about twenty minutes. We were already on our way to the Milan airport when Danny's sister called the hotel from North Carolina to say his mother had collapsed at work and was in the hospital on the intensive care ward. The prognosis was not good; she needed immediate heart-bypass surgery, or else.

My parents gave us the news when we returned to New York and went over to their apartment to pick up Mae. Danny called North Carolina from their apartment and got all of the ruthless details. We decided it would save time and worry if he just went straight back to the airport and flew down to Winston-Salem on the next flight, alone. If he had to stay there for a while, then Mae and I could always join him later. For now, his getting there fast was all that mattered.

Trouble always knows how to take you by nasty surprise. One minute you're sitting at home by the fire, then—*blink*—you're suddenly in a completely foreign city where you don't speak the language, all the banks are closed, you've got no map and night's already come.

My parents asked if I wanted to stay there with them, but after Danny left I was too hyper and out-of-sorts to accept their offer. I just wanted to put Mae in her playpen by the sunny window in our living-room, get out of my squashed travelling clothes, shower, look at the mail . . . be home.

It was a big mistake not to stay with the folks. As usual, my parents had treated Miss Mae James like the belle of the ball and she was not about to relinquish *that* status willingly. In other words, she was a complete pill for the rest of the day. Welcome home, Mommy! We glared daggers at each other until she finally gave up in gasping fury and went to sleep in her crib with an impressive snarl on her face.

Later, Eliot called from downtown to say hello and how was it? When I told him what was going on, he said he'd come by in a couple of hours with dinner from our local horrible Chinese restaurant. I was so glad to hear his voice and know he'd be there to keep me company. Before that, the evening ahead had looked awfully long and forlorn.

My inner time clock was so whacked out that after his phone call, my whole system started shutting down whether I liked it or not. I knew it was nap time.

The phone woke me. When I opened my eyes, everything in the room was dark beyond shadows. The ringing was shrill and bitter.

Alarmed, I looked at my watch and its green glow told me I had slept over three hours.

As I struggled off the couch, still drugged from sleep, I banged into Eliot who was coming in from the kitchen on tiptoes with a burbling Mae in his arms. I was so surprised to see him there that I let out a whoop that scared all of us.

'It's only me, Cullen! Get the phone!'

Danny was calling from his sister's house; his mother was very weak, but stable. The surgery would be performed in the morning if everything was still all right; her chances of making it were good.

'What do you mean by "good", Dan?'

'Better than fifty-fifty, the doctor said. Did you call Eliot?'

'He's right here now. Are you okay, Danny?'

'No, Cul, I'm scared and I'm worried. But what can you expect?'

I loved him for saying that, and not, 'Everything's okay. I'm tough as nails.' Because Danny *was* tough, but this wasn't the time to play virile and swagger around. It was the time to pray and be scared and feel very small.

'Can I do anything for you, love?'

I felt his smile through the telephone. 'Give Mae a big squeeze for me and tell her I'll be home soon. I'll call you tomorrow as soon as I know.'

We said goodbye without really wanting to, but there was nothing else to say. Eliot moved around the room, turning on lights.

'So do you want to talk first, or do you want to eat? I got spring rolls and monk's food.'

'Eliot, I'm sure glad you're here tonight.'

He nodded and smiled. 'Me too. Let's eat and then you can tell me all about Milan. Was it marvellous? What did I miss?'

5

It was no longer hard to keep pace with Mr Tracy. He walked with great difficulty on three legs and tired much too easily. The snow slowed him even more.

Pepsi and I wore rough parkas made out of perlmoos hides stitched crudely and haphazardly together. They were ugly as sin and smelled like pumpkin pie, but they kept us very warm and protected against storms which never seemed to end from one day to the next.

We were crossing the Brotzhool, Rondua's equivalent to the Alps. Thankfully, there was no real climbing involved—only slogging up and down mountain passes on snowshoes the size of road signs.

Here was our caravan—Mr Tracy led the way, with four negnugs walking directly under him to protect them from the snow. I had no idea why they'd chosen to accompany us this far, but we were certainly glad of it. They were serious little fellows who didn't do a whole lot of joking around, but they kept careful watch over us in their fashion. Much more importantly, they knew every step of the way we were taking.

Mr Tracy *let* them lead us and that worried me greatly. Since the calamity with Martio and the loss of his leg, the dog's whole being flapped like a big flag in a small wind. Whether it was because he had lost his loved and trusted friends, or his leg, or simply the desire to go on, Mr Tracy had become a kind of tired stranger who wasn't interested in very much of anything. Whenever we stopped for the night, he stayed by us physically but at the same time retreated so far into himself that we could barely reach him. And after many days and as many attempts, we didn't try.

On the other side of the Brotzhool was Jack Chili. Our job was to

147

get there, face him, fight (I assumed) and try to defeat him. None of us said anything about that part of the journey, but who needed to? We had enough evidence of his capabilities. Plus, since he didn't have to pretend to be Martio the Camel any more, Chili proved how creative he was when it came to malevolence.

An example? Every night the negnugs led us to different mountain huts where we could stay. They said Stastny Panenka built all of them when he and his Battle Dogs crossed the Brotzhool centuries before, while searching for the Perfumed Hammer. Both Pepsi and I were so weary when we heard that explanation that neither of us asked for an elaboration on either Stastny or his Hammer.

All of us were shocked the first time we entered one of these huts, because inside was a cosy, bustling fire in the fireplace and a beautiful meal laid out for us on a table in the middle of the room. But that hut, and all subsequent ones, was empty.

This happened for a week, at places ten or fifteen miles distant from each other. It was very nice, but also uncomfortable and too mysterious. I found myself eating fast and checking over my shoulder after a while.

On the ninth or tenth night, we opened a wooden door on to much the same scene. This time, set in the middle of the dining table, was Mr Tracy's leg—cooked, and garnished with sprigs of parsley.

A zeppelin began following us. One morning we walked out of a hut and there, incredibly, it was. The kind of dinosaur-like blimp that you see hovering over football stadiums when there's a big game on. Only this blimp flew so low and close to us that the whirr of its black motors could be clearly heard. It scared the hell out of me. How it ever managed to manoeuvre around in such tight, rocky quarters was impossible to say. But it did, and never went away from that day on. We had no idea who was flying it, or why they were there.

Our singular band made it across the mountains intact, but we certainly weren't Hannibal and his boys thundering down out of the Alps on golden elephants, ripe for battle with whoever. Mr Tracy had inconceivably lost his mystical hat and even Pepsi walked with a limp as a result of sliding half-way down an ice-field one memorable morning.

We came off the last broad tongue of snow into one of those great green mountain meadows where fat calm cows grazed. The smell of high pine, ice and wet earth was everywhere—the wind's perfume and gift.

I lay down and put both arms over my face. When I woke half an hour later, I heard laughing and fast conversation. What welcome sounds after so many days of silence and worry! Propping myself up on my elbows, I turned to Pepsi and Mr Tracy and saw they were talking with an *exquisite* looking man in a tuxedo and white silk gloves. Even Mr Tracy looked happier and less done in. He was nodding at whatever the stranger was saying. When Pepsi looked my way, his eyes were all little-boy joyous.

'Mom, Stastny Panenka's here with all of his men. They were the guys in the blimp. They're here to help us!'

The man got up and walked over. Taking my hand, he closed his eyes, kissed the tips of my fingers and bowed. What a gent.

'*Drovo pradatsch, Zulbi. Tras-treetsch.*'

'Pepsi, would you come here? I don't know what he's saying.'

Before he came, Pepsi held a hurried conference with Mr Tracy. The big dog listened more than he spoke. When they were finished, Pepsi took the familiar first Bone out of his knapsack and brought it over with him.

'Close your eyes, Mom.'

Putting the Bone firmly against my throat, he said something mellifluous but impossible to make out, as usual. Then he did the same thing to each of my ears.

'You'll understand everyone now, Mom. Later it'll go away because you're really not supposed to have this power, but for now you'll understand. You'd better get ready because it comes fast.'

The experience was similar to entering a railway station or airport from a silent corridor or street. Instantly, absolutely everything around me had a voice and was using it every second. The grass spoke of the fickleness of the wind, the clouds of their search for the perfect speed across the sky. Stones, flowers, insects . . . All of them talked over and under and beyond each other in a kind of pleasant cacophony of original voices I had never heard in Rondua, much less imagined existed.

One of my favourite books when I was a little girl was *Doctor Doolittle,* but I was envious of his ability to speak the language of Gub-Gub the pig, or laugh at the jokes of horses. How wonderful it felt at this new moment to be able to laugh at the jokes of everything!

After the initial tidal wave of racket, I learned to filter out most of the sounds so that I could pay attention to the lovely-looking Stastny Panenka.

'Vuk and Zdravko will be coming in from the First Stroke any day now. That I am sure of. The problem we have is Endaxi and his Barking Flutes . . . You never know with them. Look, when you have ten brothers all married to the same woman, you cannot expect them to be dependable! I'm sorry about that. They are good fighters. If they come, they come.'

Looking proudly at his zeppelin off in the near distance (which seemed to be grazing the sky as calmly as the cows, directly below it, grazed the meadow), he rattled off the names of others who would be joining us on our march against Jack Chili.

The only thing that made an impression on me was the name/word 'Endaxi'. Endaxi meant 'O.K.' in Greek. 'Do you want another coke?' 'Endaxi.' The question was, in Rondua, who was Endaxi and his Barking Flutes? Within the next few days we were to find out.

'They look like fire-bees, huh, Mom?'

We had been on a night cruise with Stastny in his blimp and were just returning to the meadow where all of our allies were massed. Hundreds of feet below, camp-fires burned everywhere. Their flickers and jumps did remind me of fire-flies, in a way.

Looking down there with Pepsi alongside reminded me of the first day we had arrived in Rondua. How much had we changed since then? In the faint light of the cockpit, I looked hard at my son's profile. His hair was longer and his face was thinner. It was too dim to see his expression, but memory told me it was as vital and open as it had been so many long days ago when we looked out of another high window in the sky and saw giant animals waiting for us below: Mr Tracy, Felina. Martio.

But what waited below us now really defied description.

They had come from every part of Rondua: from cities, hives, forests, towers, nests, caves, under rocks, jungles, deep water . . . They had come to join us because it was known everywhere that this would be the final battle, the final chance to do what one could to save a world that otherwise was truly lost. Final battles are not a new thing in the history of the world, but they are still more terrible than anything else. They are the last resort, and only the desperate or the mad ever revert to that. When an entire civilization is pushed to that extreme, nothing could be more dangerous.

'Would you like to stay up here for a while? We have plenty of gas and everything seems to be under control below.'

Pepsi shook his head and said there was too much work to do down there before we went to sleep. Stastny quickly gave orders for the eel ladders to be let down. Whatever my son said now, Ronduans hopped to it with an alacrity that shocked me. Had he suddenly, or secretly, become someone I wasn't aware of? Sure, he was Pepsi with the Four Bones, but he had had them an awfully long time and no one had made such a big deal of it before. What had happened? Or rather, what *was* happening to change Rondua's attitude towards him? Was it the imminence of both Jack Chili and our forthcoming battle with him?

An hour before, while out cruising the night skies, Stastny had pointed without any big fanfare to a small sparsely-lit village in one of the mountain valleys about ten miles from our meadow.

'That's it. That's where he lives.'

'Jack Chili? Down *there?*' From up in the sky, the town looked as if it had barely two hundred houses, if that.

'Yes, down there.'

'But I don't see anything! It looks totally asleep. Where are all of his troops and forces, or whatever you call them?'

'Still in the children's heads.' Stastny spoke as if I should have known that.

'What are you talking about?'

We motored on for two or three minutes more before Panenka ordered all engines stopped. Pressing a button on one of the glowing red consoles, he brought a brilliant spotlight to life on the left side of the gondola. Shining it back and forth on the ground below, he finally found what he was looking for: a long building set back on the side of a hill in the middle of a thick forest. In that stark unnatural light, the place looked like a bandage on the hill's dark head.

'What's that?'

'The Café Deutschland.'

'What do you mean, *café?*' It did *not* look like a place where you drank coffee.

'Jack Chili gives names to things. Half the time no one knows what they mean except him. He calls that the Café Deutschland. It's a madhouse for children.'

'My God. What does he do to them?' I shivered as if someone had put a cold hand on the back of my neck.

'To the children? Nothing at all. Don't misunderstand. It's reputed to be very clean and pleasant inside. The children are treated very well.'

'*And?*'

'And . . . Chili is able to use the children's nightmares. He taps into what they dream and chooses the parts which he wants to bring into being.'

'You mean, one of those poor mad children has a dream—'

Stastny interrupted me with a gentle defeated voice and a hand on my arm. A small squeeze. 'A mad child dreams terrible things, doesn't it? Jack Chili enters their sleep, chooses whatever he wants in their dreams, and then those things become his soldiers.'

'My God! There's no way we'll ever win! Against that? Kids' nightmares? *Mad* kids? Big bugs with six heads? Rats on fire? Things from horror movies multiplied a thousand times?' I was getting louder and louder, but I couldn't help it. 'That's our enemy? Stastny, we're talking about Hell here. If you just take a *normal* kid's imagination—'

'Mom, would you be quiet?'

'All right. I'm sorry.'

'Let's go home, Stastny.'

The many camp-fires on the meadow were reassuring in a small way, but what we'd learned sixty minutes ago was enough to leave anyone in drop-jawed paralysis. The entire ride back, I sat silently in my seat, masochistically trying to remember some of the nightmares *I* had had as a child.

Once on the ground again, I asked Stastny if I could speak to Pepsi alone.

'Honey, do you know what you're doing? Do you know what you're *going* to do?'

'I think so, Mom. But first I have to talk with Mr Tracy to make sure it's all right.'

'Can you tell me?'

'I'm sorry, Mom, no.'

He was facing me and I couldn't resist reaching out to brush the flop of hair off his forehead. 'That's okay, Peps. Did you know that you're getting to be a very handsome guy?' He took my hand and, turning away from the zeppelin, pulled me along after him.

We wove in and around groups of people and creatures who greeted us warmly when we passed, like old friends or comrades-in-arms. They could fly and swim and run impossibly fast. They carried weapons of cunning design that were capable of every wound; of splitting hearts behind any steel.

There was such a good, united feeling everywhere; no buzz of fear or hesitation, and much laughter. I must admit though that to hear the laughter of some of our stranger . . . allies was, well, disconcerting.

'Cullen! Hey, Cullen, over here!' I looked hard into the dark and thought I saw Weber Gregston waving to me from a camp-fire, but I couldn't be certain. I wanted to stop and find out for sure, but Pepsi had my hand and he was in a hurry.

There were also all kinds of music there, which was queer and lovely and often spellbinding. Time after time I wanted to stop and listen to this voice or these wings rubbed together. There was an instrument that looked like a microscope which sounded like nothing I had ever heard before anywhere.

But Pepsi wouldn't stop. He jerked me along and seemed impatient when I asked him again and again what that last song was, or the name of the being that was playing it.

Mr Tracy had moved very little since the day we'd arrived on the meadow. They had erected a tent the size of a circus marquee for us and he spent most of his time inside either resting or, when he was up to it, conferring with leaders of the different groups which had gathered.

When we got to the tent, an old friend of ours was there.

'Goosemasks and coffee, Venice Dancers.'

'Sizzling Thumb!'

Beaming, the old man turned and greeted us by waving the Bone-walking stick we had given to him. And because of the recent magic I'd been given, I could finally understand what he was talking about.

'Did your mother see it?'

'Yes, everything.'

I looked at the boy. 'Pepsi, did you know about the Café before?'

'Yes Mom, but I had never seen it. I'd only heard about it from Mr Tracy.'

'Did you recognize anything, Cullen?'

'No. Should I have?'

The three of them passed looks back and forth that said I damned well should have recognized everything.

I got mad. 'All right! I give up. What did I miss this time?'

Using the walking stick to steady himself, Sizzling Thumb got up slowly. All humour and goodwill was gone from his face as he came up close and looked hard at me.

'How could you forget that? That's where the others *died*, Cullen! On that hill, when you were all so close.' He wanted to say more, but anger or self-control kept him from continuing.

Taking him by the arm, Pepsi led him out of the tent. It was the last time I ever saw Sizzling Thumb and I have no idea of what happened to him. When he was gone, Mr Tracy told me that Sizzling Thumb's only children, Umleitung and Tookat, had been killed in that battle. The day I used the fourth Bone to save myself! How well I understood his rage then. Long ago but not far away I had caused the deaths of his family, and now I didn't even remember that happening.

'Mr Tracy, if I don't remember anything, what good will I be when the fighting starts?'

He thought for a moment and was about to answer when Pepsi came running into the tent.

'Mom, come outside!' His voice and expression said to drop everything and come running.

One of the few dreams I distinctly remember having as a child was this, and I had it many times. I am sitting outside somewhere by myself. It is a nice day and I'm doing something unimportant— maybe a doll is on my lap and I'm talking to it. For no reason, I feel compelled to look up and there, owning the entire sky—the whole roof and corners of the world above—is a face. I'm scared, but children have the ability to handle anything because their world has no limitations: everything is possible when you're eight. So this face across the world is incredible, but not out of the question. Is it God? I don't know, because I don't remember what the face looked like; just that it was everywhere above me. It is the face of a man; he never speaks but he is looking only at me. The air smells peppery and rich and anything might happen. I wake up.

Dashing out of the tent behind Pepsi, I smelled it first—peppery and rich. Night had been swept aside by a brilliantly lit sky which was once again taken up by one horizon-to-horizon face. There

154

were so many hundreds of our friends down in that meadow but even combined, they were as microbes in comparison with that omnipotent face. When he spoke, his voice was soft and lovely.

'Remember me?'

6

Dear Mrs James,

    You will be delighted to know that this is my last letter to you. I am having to resort to paying a certain person to take it out of the hospital and mail it to you. I assume just this once you will have the 'kindness' not to report it to the good Doctor Lavery.

    He has explained your decision to me and I understand, but it makes me unhappy. No, to be more precise, it makes me feel horrible, if you care to know the truth. I thought you were the only person left in the world I could rely on. I guess we all make mistakes, don't we? I am sorry, I feel horrible, but that's all right. I will respect your decision and honour it. That is what a shogun would do. Doctor Lavery suggested I begin a diary to compensate for the loss of my correspondence with you, and I believe that I will do that. I find writing helps me to express my thoughts more clearly, whether *you* have been aware of that or not. The only problem with a journal is that you're the only one to read it, so you can't get any feedback because you usually agree with everything you said. Ha Ha! Goodbye, Mrs James. Thank you for almost something, if you understand what I mean. Yes, you do know what I mean, don't you?

Very sincerely yours,
Alvin Williams

'Oh, light your cigarette with it, Cullen. Alvin Williams is a nut.'

    'Do you think I should call his doctor and tell him about it?'

    'I guess you could if you want to, but I wouldn't bother. Alvin is mad at you, that's all. But mad people *get* mad. I say screw him.'

    'Eliot, you're oversimplifying by a few miles.'

    'Then call the doctor if you want. I don't know what else to tell you.' He smoothed the hair over Mae's head and shifted her from one arm to the other. 'Enough of loony Alvin. Are you going to tell me the new Rondua dream or not?'

'Well, this is all part of it. I'm kind of scared to tell it to you.'

'Why?'

'Because the face across the sky was Alvin Williams' face. *He's* Jack Chili.'

'Hah, that's perfect! You're like a casebook history, Cullen. You keep thinking that dreaming about Rondua is bad for you, but you're so wrong. Some little catharsis-faucet inside you turns on each night and you get to wash away every bit of guilt and fear and . . . everything bad in your life from Day One until now. By the time you get through this whole thing, you'll probably be able to *ascend*, for God's sake!' He tsked his lips at me and shook his head. 'It's disgusting, because it's all so neat and completely logical. What's the worst thing in the world you can imagine happening to you? Having to face Alvin Williams again. Now, you go to sleep at night and who is it you're terrified of facing in your dreams? Alvin Williams, multiplied a thousand times. And who are you going to *have* to face? Alvin Williams. Cullen, you would have bored Sigmund Freud in ten seconds. *The White Hotel* you're not. And anyway, what happened after Alvin Chili appeared in the sky?'

The name Alvin Chili made me laugh and that cleared the air.

'Alvin Chili told us we had to come alone to him. Just the two of us. He said it was either that or else he would kill everyone in the meadow right then.'

'Even that makes sense. Stop looking at me like that, Cullen! You took literature courses in college, didn't you? Well, quest stories are always like that. Big armies go out to fight, but in the end it always boils down to just one against one. King Arthur, Beowulf and Grendel, even *Lord of the Rings* . . . they're all the same. There's a final, *final* pitched battle that decides everything and it's only between the hero and maybe, at most, one or two of his Musketeer buddies. In your case, it's Pepsi and you against Jack Chili, alias Axe Boy Williams.'

I got up and walked from here to there and back again. It did no good.

'There's something else too.'

'What?'

'Eliot, you've never once told me the names of any of your lovers, have you?'

157

'No. Is it important? Do you want to know?'

'You don't have to tell me. Wyatt Leonard. André Ronig. Shaw Ballard.'

'Jesus, how do you know that? Did you have me tailed?'

'I didn't have to. Eliot, I just *know.* I suddenly know all of these things that I don't *want* to know. Listen to me. Danny's mother is going to get better, but the day after tomorrow they'll have a big scare with her at the hospital because of her operation and Danny will have to stay down there another ten days.'

'What else?'

'What else? Things, Eliot. Little *hors d'oeuvres* of the future, things now. Your lovers' names, things like that. Remember you said you thought I had powers? That that's how I knocked down Weber? Well, you're right. I have them. I can do things I don't want to do. I guess I really did zap Weber. Then I took the zap off him with a magic word. Then there was the gypsy woman in Milan. How's this —your friend Wyatt Leonard is going to be fired in a month. But he thinks he's going to get a raise.'

'Shit!'

'That's right, Eliot. Shit.'

'Do you see anything bad, Cullen? Is anyone going to die or anything?'

'I don't know; that's not there. Or maybe it is, but I haven't seen it yet. I don't have any control over this—it all comes like a big wind and blows me over. I saw a man in the street today who is about to inherit a thousand dollars from an uncle he hated. I knew that, but I didn't even know what the guy's name was. There are always gaps in whatever comes to me, I never see the whole picture of anything.'

'What about the stock market?'

'Don't be stupid, Eliot.'

'I'm not. Do you know how many people with the kind of powers you're talking about have lived? Lots! They had them and they got used to them. They had to, it was as simple as that.'

'Bullshit, Eliot! It's not simple, and you *don't* get used to them. You don't shoot purple beams of killer light out of your hand . . . You don't dream about a Rondua night after night and get used to it.'

'You do! You're going to have to, Cullen; whether your powers and Rondua are linked or not. Like it or not, it's all you, honey, and you can't pull those things out of you like bad teeth.'

158

'I know. I want to show you something else. Have you got a cigarette?'

I lit up and let it burn down part way before I began. 'Watch this.' Taking a big drag, I rounded my lips to blow a smoke-ring. Puff. The ring came rolling out, a smoky-grey doughnut. Five inches from my mouth, it came together and formed a perfect little car which drove across the room at eye level until it disappeared in the air.

'What would you like next, Eliot? A truck? A snail? Any requests? How about a pug dog like Zampano?'

It was easy. My copy of Eliot's dog came out and ran across the air after the car.

'Hey there, Foxy Lady. How'd you like to fuck a champion?'

I looked at the man and gave him my angriest scowl. 'Go away, will you?'

My arms were full of groceries and I was half a block from home. Mae was in the apartment listening to Beatles records with Eliot while he finished a review for his newspaper.

'Hey, you think I got herpes? No way, beautiful! Come on, I'll show you moves your husband doesn't know. Listen, I'm a sex instructor. First lesson free.'

'Leave me alone. Drift. *Die.* Okay? Just leave me alone.' I should have kept my mouth shut and just kept walking straight ahead.

Moving alongside me, the creep put his hand on my elbow and squeezed it like it was a melon on sale at the market. 'Don't go so fast, sweetie. You and me gotta talk. You're a super fox, you know that? I think you dialled my number.'

I stopped and looked at him. A black beret, dirty 'Stanford University' sweat-shirt, dirty black sweat-pants, dirty green sneakers with pink laces.

'What's your name, Scuzzball?'

'Hey, now we're talking. I knew you was cool. My name ain't Scuzzball; it's Swift. All my good friends call me Swift, little lady. What's yours?'

'Look at your hand, Swift. Watch it carefully.'

The fingers quickly undid their crabbed grip on my elbow and started leaping around in the air. It looked as if they were trying to play an invisible piano. One down, the next up, next down. I blinked my eyes and made them go faster. *Faster.*

'What's this shit?' He tried to move away.

'Stand still, Swift.'

I made his arm rise high above his head. His hand, the fingers still playing, went round and round in quick wild circles. I made him do that too.

'Cut it out, man! Fuck off! Lemme go!'

I was so calm. 'Now look at your other hand, Swiftie.' Up it went. 'Now, keep them right there. Right where they are. I'll see you later, okay?'

He screamed at me as I walked away. When I got to our building, I let him go.

'Eliot, I liked it. I *liked* being able to do that to him!'

'So what? I would too, Cullen. Don't sound so guilty. The little scum deserved it and we both know it. "Wanna fuck a champion." God, what dreck! I've been trying to tell you all along it can work to your benefit. You should be thankful you have it.'

We were in a cab going downtown—Mae too. A splashy new restaurant called 'The Future of Lightning' had opened on Third Avenue in the sixties and was the talk of all the glossy magazines. Danny had called earlier and, as predicted, said his mother had had a setback; he would have to stay a little longer in North Carolina. Our conversation was to the point and entirely too brief. The sound of my husband's quiet, solid voice reminded me once again how much I liked to chat with him. Schmoozing was a favourite hobby of ours, and when we hadn't had a good gab for a while, life wasn't as much fun. This was the first time we had been separated for any length of time since we'd been together, and I was really taken aback to find how hollow parts of my day were without Dan around.

Just before we hung up, he suggested that since he couldn't be there to take me, why didn't I invite Eliot out to dinner somewhere. I said I would and both of us waited for the other to hang up after we'd said goodbye.

Conversations with Danny were a long wander through familiar greatly-loved countryside. Talking with Eliot, on the other hand, was like an evening spent in a kerbside chair at a hopping Italian restaurant. His words and ideas buzzed in and out like kids on orange scooters—in a hurry everywhere. Gusts of noise, colour, honking, crazy combinations that often left you ga-ga. Little of it ever

160

slowed down enough for you to really focus on, but the happy frenzy did your heart good.

'Cullen, stop looking at me so damned sceptically! Do you think I have a green head? Mae, your mother has *several* levels to go before she reaches enlightenment.'

'I'm not sceptical, Eliot, I'm just worried. What if these powers or whatever get stronger? Do you know what I've been thinking about all day? Remember *The Sorcerer's Apprentice,* the Walt Disney cartoon? The sorcerer goes out for a while and leaves his magic wand lying around; his apprentice picks it up and—'

'—And he doesn't know how to control it and disaster strikes! You're talking about one of my favourite films, Cullen. Don't you think I had a childhood too? Listen, how many times do I have to tell you—if your powers get stronger, then you wait to see what *kind* of stronger and take it from there.'

A little surprisingly, he touched my cheek and ran one finger down to my chin. 'Always remember too that I'm around if you need my help.'

I took his hand, squeezed it and gently bit the finger. 'I know you are, pal. And I'm really happy you are, too.'

The decor of 'The Future of Lightning' was chic-Zen monastery: stripped and sealed wood floors in a nice herringbone pattern, no-nonsense white tables and bentwood chairs, an incongruous rock garden in the middle of it all. A big potted palm off in one corner looked strangely forlorn and out of place.

'Cullen, don't look now but . . . check who's over there to the left.'

Weber Gregston held a spare-rib in one hand and gestured with it while he talked to the beautiful and famous June Sillman, the star of *Sorrow and Son.* That first unexpected sight of him sent goose-pimples over my skin like a searchlight over the ocean.

The maître d' showed us to a table on the other side of the room. It was just as well because I didn't know how I felt about talking to him, even after everything that had happened.

'How do you feel, Cullen?'

'Kind of funny. I'd like to talk to him, but there's a part of me that doesn't want to at all. Maybe he'll just add to my complications.'

Mae chose that moment to pick up my water glass and throw it on the floor. *Crash!* Thank you, Mae. A waiter moved right in to clean up the mess, but the noise had been loud and drawn a lot of eyes.

'He's com-ing!'

'So he's coming? Don't make me feel uncomfortable, Eliot.'

'Hi, Weber.'

'Hi, Eliot. Hi, Mae James. Hi, Mom James.' He patted Mae on the head, then came around the table and kissed me. 'Where the hell have you been? Every time I call you no one's home.'

'My husband and I were in Italy for a few days. We just got back.'

'Okay—listen, you and I have got to talk about something. It's about this dream I had the other night.' His face was so serious it made me fidgety and he looked at Eliot to see if he was in on the whole Rondua thing.

'I know about the dreams, Weber. She told me everything.'

'Good, then let me tell you what happened.' He started to sit down, but saw Eliot gesture with his head towards Weber's table, where June Sillman was sitting alone now and not looking too happy.

'June can wait a few minutes. This dream can't. Cullen, do you know Fire Sandwich yet? Have you met him?'

'No.'

'He says he knows you. He said he's a friend of Squeeny.'

'Who's Squeeny, Weber?'

'You don't know him either?'

'Nope. Never heard of either of them.'

'All right, that doesn't even matter. I stopped dreaming about Rondua about two weeks ago. The dreams were coming hard and fast, night after night, but then one night they just stopped and then there weren't any more. I didn't understand it—they're there a hundred per cent one night, and then the next they're gone for good. And I haven't had another since then. Rondua's left my head for ever, I think. But the last dream I had, Cullen, was a doozie. There were big battles and strange animals . . . You know what I'm talking about. Anyway, I talked to this one guy named Fire Sandwich. He said you were going to have to fight Jack Chili and that Chili knew how to beat you.'

'I already know that, Weber.'

He was about to say something, but stopped and looked at me strangely. 'So you know about your son too? About what happens to him?'

162

'What? What are you talking about?'
'Do you really want me to tell you?'
'Yes, of course.'
'He dies.'

7

Leaving Mr Tracy was easier to do than I had imagined. The three of us walked silently across the now-empty meadow. All of the others were gone: the silver zeppelin, the music, the exotic languages and laughter around the hundreds of camp-fires. The safety of our numbers had gone home to await the outcome of our final confrontation with Jack Chili.

'I wish there was something more I could do to help you, Pepsi. Not so long ago I thought I had some power, but our friend Martio showed me I was wrong about that.'

'Do you think my plan will work, Mr Tracy?'

'No. I told you that before and I don't even know why you are going to try. Jack Chili is too blind and rancorous to see your point, Pepsi. You're completely right; Rondua could work the way you've suggested, but he'll never understand that way of thinking.' The dog's voice was all defeat.

No matter what happened to us, I was convinced that Mr Tracy would die soon, either because this fear had grown into a cancer or simply because he was just plain used-up. There seemed so little left in him that, to a certain degree, I was glad to be leaving before life rushed in to close on him right in front of us. His strength and courage had buoyed us up for so long. To see him without any of those things now was enough to make you fatally sad.

'You remember the route, Pepsi? Follow the Dead Handwriting until you come to the Hot Shoes. Carmesia knows the way, but you'll leave her at the Shoes and then the two of you will be on your own.'

Pepsi nodded and without another word, turned to leave. His face was twisted as if it had just been cut with a knife. I couldn't say goodbye that way. I went up to Mr Tracy and put my arms as far around his neck as I could. The tears began before I got the first word out.

'Goodbye, Mr Tracy. I love you. I love you very much.'

'Goodbye, Cullen. Do whatever you can for the boy. Then stand back and the rest will be up to him. It's his job now; you've done yours. He's a very good boy.' With the slightest movement of his leg, he pushed me away. Then he turned and began to limp back to the tent. I could feel his steps through the ground. I watched him until my heart hurt too much. Luckily, Carmesia the negnug marched up below me and said we had to get going—Pepsi was already 'under way'.

We came to a valley that was jade green on one side, sheer black rock-face on the other. Carved everywhere into the rock were mammoth letters and numbers, enigmatical words, sketches of half-completed things: animals, futuristic buildings and furniture and structures the likes of which I had never seen in Rondua, almost-human faces. The Dead Handwriting. Like those mysterious stone faces on Easter Island, no one in Rondua knew where the Handwriting came from. According to Carmesia, many thought it was one of the early gods doodling while he tried to think up what he wanted to do next with Rondua.

While we stared, Carmesia bent to the ground and started sniffing all over the place like a hunting dog hot on the track of something. Pepsi and I looked at each other, both equally mystified.

'The heat comes from up ahead; I can smell its direction. The Shoes should be very close.'

Everything seemed very simple now. Pass the Hot Shoes (whatever they were), say goodbye to Carmesia the negnug, then walk straight on until we came to Jack Chili and whatever horrors he had waiting for us.

I once watched a documentary on animals in Africa. Beside the usual vaulting gazelles and funny-looking outraged hippos, there was one part of the film that left me reeling when it was over. A lion, slim and airborne all the way, chased a zebra across a plain and won. Grabbing the zebra by the nose, the lion shook it back and forth like a rag. It was hard to watch, God knows, but the most awesome thing about the picture was the zebra's reaction. Once caught, it stood stock-still and allowed itself to be devoured. The

165

film's narrator calmly said that brutal as it might appear to us, nature had actually provided a merciful device for this final moment. The zebra stood so still because its system had already shut off. It had gone into such complete shock that, so far as scientists could figure, it felt nothing from then on despite what was actually happening to it.

Watching my feet follow Pepsi's, I wondered if the same kind of shock had set in in me. I was wary of our precarious future, but not so afraid now. Was that because I had grown up some; got stronger along the way to the fifth Bone of the Moon? Or was this new unruffled me a result of knowing Jack Chili had both Pepsi and I by the nose, and there was little we could do now beside watch ourselves be destroyed? Shock, or a transcendent bravery I had never experienced in myself before?

The Dead Handwriting stopped suddenly although the rock face, bare of anything but nature's streaks and scratches, continued. The path was very narrow and kept us walking in tight single file, Carmesia leading the way. The stones under our feet were smooth and flat and made for a lot of slipping and sliding if you didn't watch where you were going. After a while it dawned on me what the 'stones' were—bottle glass, all of them the same colour as the piece I had found on the beach in Greece.

While walking, I somehow started thinking about the trams in Milan; how I had always loved the names of their destinations: Greece, Brazil, Tirana. If there was nothing to do on a sunny day, I used to climb aboard one, sit down and—closing my eyes—tell myself I was off to Brazil. Just like that! Later, if I was meeting Danny at our favourite café across from the Castello Sforzesco, he would inevitably see a certain look in my eye and ask, 'Where did you go today, Captain?' And I would be able to say, 'Hungary'.

From our apartment near the Castello, we could hear the busy clank/clack of them passing all day and deep into the night. I loved them. Somehow their loud welcome sound always said to me, 'This is Europe. We live only in Europe.'

The bottle-glass path turned a sharp corner and directly ahead were six glowing orange shoes, two storeys high at the very least. They were men's Oxford shoes and were connected to tweed-covered legs as thick and high as California redwood trees that climbed up and through the clouds. None of these legs moved. I should have been afraid of them, but I wasn't. The zebra and the lion?

166

The heat from the glowing shoes increased as we got closer. When Carmesia stopped, Pepsi reached into his knapsack and brought out the third and fourth Bones. He handed me the third.

'Hold it very tight against your chest when we pass them, Mom. It'll protect you.'

Carmesia stood between us. 'I have to go back now, Pepsi.'

Pepsi reached down and picked up the negnug. For the first time I realized the boy understood their language as well. When we'd first met the little animals by the Sea of Brynn, he hadn't been able to do so.

'Carmesia, be sure to tell Mr Tracy that the shoes aren't moving. That'll make him feel better. But also tell him we got this far and everything's okay from what I've seen. Goodbye. Thank you!' He kissed the thing on the top of its head and put it gently down on the ground. It gave a stiff military salute and then skittered away back up the trail. It moved so fast that it was gone in no time at all.

Touching the fourth Bone to his chest, Pepsi gestured with his head for me to follow. The crack of rocks moving around underfoot followed us as we moved towards the Shoes—the Shoes that radiated like some kind of big, cockamamie spaceship from Planet Foot.

Holding the Bone hard against my chest, I still felt the heat of the Shoes, but only distantly, as if they were somehow much further off. As we got closer to them, the glass stones beneath our feet glowed all kinds of different fiery colours.

When we were almost all the way past the Hot Shoes, Pepsi dropped his Bone down the front of his shirt and to my horror, walked straight over to the last of these orange Goliaths. Climbing slowly up over its perforated toe, he made his way to the top by grabbing sections of the laces and putting his feet in the brass lace-holes at the sides. If watching that wasn't enough to bring on a heart-attack, once he reached the top of the Shoe he climbed on to the sock and made his way vertically up its fuzzy, sheer face. I kept squinting my eyes so that I wouldn't have to see everything so clearly. Once when he lost his handhold and almost fell, I turned away . . . but not for long.

The worst moment came when, after climbing out and over the cuff of one pants leg, he actually disappeared down inside it. At that point, all six of the Shoes sent off a flare of molten orange light which blinded me momentarily. Oh, God! Eyes gone, I started screaming for Pepsi. By the time my eyesight had fully returned, I saw him scampering down the Shoe again with a smile a yard wide on his face.

'What were you *doing?*'

He came up and hugged me tightly; his head came to the bottom of my waist. 'I can't tell you yet, Mom. Wait till later.'

And then we were off again on what turned out to be the last part of our journey. Eliot would have called it our quest.

We sat on a bottle-glass boulder and watched fog float gloomily across the valley below. Gloomy was the word for everything at the moment, because on the other side of that partially-hidden valley was the Café Deutschland, Jack Chili, etcetera. We were waiting for the fog to lift because a few miles back, the path had turned steep and quirky in its twists and illogical turns. Neither of us needed a sprained ankle or twisted knee right then.

There was a part of me that wanted to ask Pepsi what *he* thought would happen when we met up with our . . . adversary over there. But this quiet moment together promised to be one of our last for a long time. Why spoil it by bringing up ugly, ominous questions that led only to threatening answers. Like: 'How do you think he'll eat us, Pepsi? With a knife and fork? Or maybe just dip us head-first into the mustard like Vienna sausages?'

'No, I don't think it'll be like that, Mom. He's already shown us he can be mean. I think he'll do something else.'

'*So,* now *you* can read my mind too?'

He looked embarrassed before he nodded.

'How often do you *do* it, young man?'

'Only when you looked worried or real scared, Mom. I promise that's the only time.'

'Hmm. Your mother does *not* appreciate having her mind read, thank you very much.'

I gave him the last of the Sidney Bean sandwiches which had been given to us before we left the meadow. Nice as that sounds, it wasn't an entirely selfless gesture on my part because I hadn't been hungry in ages. I must have eaten at times, but I certainly didn't remember where or when.

'Let's go, Mom. It looks like the fog's going away.' Like any kid, he ate his sandwich all the way down the hill and straight into the roiling fog.

168

We walked for some time before coming to the first of the children. The fog had done a good job of keeping them hidden from us.

Delicate sand-coloured wicker chairs were placed by the side of the path about every two feet or so. The children sat in them. Some had smeared, ruined features—the result of either nature's worst pranks or mad, sadistic surgeons. Black, dead-blood bruises and livid yellow and brown railway-track-like scars covered this wrecked human landscape. Some of the children looked like impossible survivors of accidents where they should have been allowed to die quickly if there was any mercy in the world. Every bit of them seemed to be either bandages, brutally exposed, or bleeding freely. A number of these shattered, blasted 'children' had apparently been propped-up, because many of them fell slowly over as we walked past.

There was no sound. No cries or screams or groans came from any of them. What made it worse was a soft, smoky-white fog which hung everywhere around us and blotted out any background that might have lessened the immediacy of the scene.

Pepsi held my hand and led me through this hell of pink-and-powder-blue pyjamas, stained gauze bandages—small bodies which should have been on swings, in sandboxes, on little bicycles that still had training wheels on the back.

'Who *are* they?'

'I think they're from the Café, Mom. Come on, keep going.'

The line of them went on and on and a moment came when I knew I couldn't stand the sight of another child, so I closed my eyes and let Pepsi lead me. But as soon as I did that, the sound of their voices and their pain came from everywhere. They called for their mothers, their fathers, for water. They wanted their brothers, their toys, the pain to stop. Everything is bigger for children, so what must their pain have been like? I kept stumbling, but that did not make me open my eyes again. Blind, my mind magnified the sound of the childrens' cries, but nothing was worse than actually seeing them. *Nothing.*

'The fog is going away, Mom. I can see way up the path.'

'How much further is there to go?'

'I don't know. There's a hill coming up that we have to take. I think it's the one that leads to the Café.'

Stumbling again, I felt the ground begin its move upwards. I squeezed Pepsi's hand and he squeezed back.

'Now it's all gone, Mom. Do you want to look?'

'No, I don't want to see the children.'

Their cries increased as the hill grew under my feet. I could feel gravity or whatever pull us backwards. How I wanted to obey that pull! Go backwards a thousand . . . a million miles until all of this was gone.

The fear and revulsion I had been so proud of conquering returned. I wondered if it was my blood that had begun to hurt everywhere inside me. But that was stupid; I hurt because I knew I was beginning to give way to panic. I hurt because I hated that; because I knew it would win. I began shaking all over my body and even my son's magical hand in mine did nothing to stop this.

'Damn it! Oh, goddamn it!' I tightened all of my muscles, then relaxed them, hoping that would help. But it didn't.

Pepsi stopped.

'What's the matter? What's wrong?'

No answer. He still didn't move. His hand had gone completely limp in mine; I had to look.

The Café Deutschland was still far away up the path, but I recognized it instantly. At first I thought its reality in front of us was what had stopped Pepsi, but that wasn't it.

Excited, but also frightened by our proximity to the infamous building, it took me some time to stop staring at it and to look again at the children. That was why Pepsi had stopped.

None of their heads was bandaged any more, although their wounds were no less horrendous. What's more, all of the bared faces were the same—Pepsi James. Pepsi without eyes, black-tumoured or gouged—or the pale green of the beaten, the jaundiced. All of them were Pepsi, all the hideous possibilities of death and almost-death on that beloved, still-recognizable face.

I was enraged. It was too much. Chili had no right to do this. It was impossible.

'You *bastard!* Come on, Pepsi. It's not real. Run and don't look at them. Take my hand!'

We ran as hard and as fast as we could. There was nothing else to do but run towards the Café.

Twenty feet away we slowed and clearly saw what was there.

Mae and I were there. I held her in my arms although we were both dead. Shining steel spikes had been driven through my forehead, my arms, and Mae as I held her. One spike went through my

170

pants at the vagina, two through my legs at the ankles. One went through Mae's temple, on and through my chest. We were recognizable, but the burst puckered flesh made us completely obscene, beyond humanity.

'Not that! No!' I dropped Pepsi's hand and bent to throw up.

When I was empty, I was just able to scratch out, 'Use the Bone, Pepsi! For God's sake, Pepsi, get us out of here, please!'

Looking up, I saw him moving away from me towards the door to the Café.

'Don't!'

He was there and I couldn't stop him from reaching behind our bodies for the door-knob. A second passed before it swung open, the bodies going with it in a slow heavy arc.

'Look, Mom!'

I couldn't see, but my son was speaking and I went to him. I followed him through the door of the Café Deutschland.

On to 90th Street and Third Avenue in New York City! My street, the street where I had lived with Danny and Mae and my life in the real world. The sight was as shocking and chilling as the wounded children, or seeing Jack Chili's face over the sky.

'Pepsi, do you know where we are?'

He turned and looked at me, all quiet eyes.

'Near your home, right, Mom?'

'But why?' I grabbed his arm much too tightly. 'What's here? How can we be here? What's going on?'

'Because Jack Chili is waiting for us in your house, Mom.'

My heart was so tired. Rubbing my hands against my sides, I wondered how far Rondua could go. How far was a dream allowed to trespass into real life, before it was caught and sent back to its proper place? Could it go haywire and take over everything you knew? Was it permitted to live wherever it wanted? Or had I alone reached a point where laws and distinctions, rules of the game, had disappeared? A point where everything in my mind, in my life, was up for grabs?

Dizzied and numb, I walked down the street with my son. I had no way to judge time, but it felt like mid-afternoon. The sun was moving towards buildings in the west, a breeze blew that had no freshness in it. Things were silent, no noise or people or signs of life anywhere. That was completely wrong and made me think this was some other 90th Street—a figment of some clever but incomplete

171

imagination. Normally my street buzzed and bustled and honked and couldn't keep still, much less stay quiet for a whole minute. It was a set for a film about to be shot: a postcard picture that looked familiar but then very wrong when you examined it more closely.

Pepsi walked slowly, taking in everything. The expression on his face went from tension to awe, to something I had never seen there before.

'Is this where you buy food, Mom?' It wasn't a question so much as a lament.

'Yes.'

'Are any of these cars yours?'

'No.'

The door to our apartment building was open and we walked in together. Another large mistake—you always, *always* needed a key to get in.

But a close friendly, *known* smell in the foyer downstairs said beyond a doubt that this was our home. Danny liked to say it was the smell of a bus station in the morning.

Danny. Oh, my Danny!

I moved quickly for the stairs, but Pepsi took my arm and shook his head. 'Go slow, Mom. I want to see your house. I want to see everything.'

Graffiti on the wall beside the bashed-in mailboxes said, 'You think this is hot? Call Barry for the real thing!' Another hand had written beneath it, 'I called, Barry, but you weren't home.'

On the second floor, I saw Eliot's door and wondered where he was in all of this. And Danny. And Mae.

At the top of the next flight of stairs, ten feet away from our door, I stopped and bit my lip. I felt the skin on my scalp tighten and move backwards on its own. I felt my heart beating all over my body—in both armpits, my throat, behind my knees, in my stomach.

Pepsi came up the last step and moved around me on to the landing. 'Are we close? Why did you stop?'

'That's our apartment, the one on the corner.'

He walked to the door and waited for me to come. I touched the door-knob. It was warm, as if someone had just rested their hand there before going in. I gave it a slight push and the door swung open, giving one metallic creak half-way that was as familiar as

172

anything I knew. Everything was familiar, yet everything was so completely, totally wrong.

Three steps through the hallway. There was the blue rug Danny had brought home one snowy night as a surprise. The Robert Munford print of lions on the walls that I looked at every day, because I liked it so much; it was one of the first things I had ever bought when I moved to New York. There was Danny's ratty old plaid umbrella that never went up right, and my green rubber raincoat—hanging next to each other on the wooden coat rack. Danny's fat black winter galoshes, one on top of the other, were on the floor. I couldn't help reaching out and touching the umbrella. It was real, it was Danny's. I was home.

Sitting on the couch in the living-room—dressed in a grey suit, white shirt and black tie—was Jack Chili, life-size this time. He was all smiles.

'Welcome home, Mrs James.' That beautiful feathery voice which I had first heard coming from the sky seemed totally obscene here.

'Don't you like my voice, Mrs James? How about something more down-home? "It's a song, Cul-len."'

Just like Danny the first time we had ever made love.

'No? Can't I be sexy too? Isn't that allowed? All right, let me think: "Oh, light your cigarette with it, Cullen."'

Eliot!

'Stop it! Those aren't your voices! You can pretend, but they're not yours.'

'*Everything* is mine, dear.' A small smile. 'All right, all right, I'll stop. Pepsi, don't you want to have a good look around before we get started? You might not get another chance later. Don't you want to see how your Mom lives? That's your sister's crib over there; that's where she sleeps.'

'Stop it!'

Without acknowledging me, he kept talking to Pepsi: 'Will you look at those little balloons on her sheets, Pepsi! Aren't they great? What do you think of that stuffed dog? His name is Odie and he's from a cartoon. Look at that terrific bed! Who'd want to grow up if they had a bed like that to sleep in? What a great place to grow up in! This is the perfect place for a kid.'

Pepsi held the top bar of Mae's crib with two tight hands and kept looking into it with sad, lost eyes.

'Why don't you fix your son a snack, Cullen? Get him a peanut

173

butter and jelly sandwich—that's his favourite. Can't you see the boy's hungry?'

Pepsi walked around the room taking it all in. He picked up a picture of Danny and me; he ran his hand over a copy of Eliot's newspaper, smiled at a white rubber dragon Mae had left on the floor. When he walked out into the hall, I made no effort to follow him. I wasn't even afraid of Jack Chili. Everything else hurt too much for there to be room inside for that. Chili and I sat there in separate silences, listening to Pepsi's feet moving slowly and quietly through the rest of our apartment.

'Don't forget to check out the pictures on the walls in the bedroom! There's a good one of Danny and Mae and your Mommy's parents—your grandparents.'

'Why don't you leave him alone? What are you going to do now?'

'*Me?* I'm not going to do anything, Cullen. It's all up to your son.' He gestured with his head towards the other room.

'What does that mean?'

'Don't worry about it. How did you like what I did with the kids' dreams back there? Great, eh? How about the quick change to their all being Pepsi? You've got to admit it was pretty effective—scared the living daylight out of you, huh? Just like the last time you were here, remember?'

He raised both hands, the old gesture of surrender, and suddenly my parents were on the floor between us. Have you ever seen a bad car accident where people have died? Or those inconceivable photographs of aeroplane crashes, mass murders, what lay at the bottom of trenches in concentration camps? Well, that is what my parents looked like, lying there on the floor in front of me: Jack Chili's latest gift. But it was clear they were very much alive and feeling every horror their bodies had been subjected to.

They made sounds . . . they moved a little.

This is what I had seen on the side of the hill leading up to the Café Deutschland, when I was a girl and first in Rondua. This is why I had used the fourth Bone of the Moon to save myself and my parents, or so I thought.

I closed my eyes. 'None of it's real.'

'No, you're wrong. It's real!'

Behind me, Pepsi entered the room and shouted something short and incomprehensible.

There was a hard *snap* and then total silence. When I looked, the

174

bodies were gone. Pepsi came up and put his hands on my shoulders. I bent my head so that I could touch a cheek to one of them.

'Thank you.'

'You little asshole! All right, all right, let's begin. Obviously you have the Bones, Pepsi, or else you couldn't have done that. Let me see them. I have to anyway.'

Pepsi sat down on the other end of the couch—Danny's seat—and slung his knapsack round into his lap. Reaching into it, he brought them out one at a time, slowly placing each one on the pillow beside him. When he was done, there were five. Five? I couldn't believe it. A fifth? Where had it come from? Where had he got the last Bone of the Moon? I looked from the five to Pepsi, to Jack Chili.

'Surprised, Mommy Cullen? You've been *had*, dearie. Your little boy's been pulling your chain.'

'I couldn't tell you, Mom—don't listen to him—I wasn't allowed to. I got it when we went to the Hot Shoes the other day. Remember when I climbed up into the pants?'

I could only nod, then I almost laughed. What bit of difference did it make? Nothing surprised me any more. Not the fifth Bone of the Moon, not my parents' bodies writhing on the floor, not Jack Chili comfortable on the couch in my living-room.

I got up and sat down again in Eliot's favourite chair; the one I'd bought at the Salvation Army and had re-covered in paisley. Just out of curiosity, I looked at the arm to see if the stain he'd made with the chocolate sundae was still there. It was. Somehow that pleased me and I covered it with my hand as if it belonged only to me.

'Do you know what happens next, Pepsi?'

'No.'

Chili sighed. 'I didn't think so. All right, I'll give you a Ronduan history lesson. Listen very carefully. No one knows these things but me, because I found the other five Bones.'

'You? *What* other five Bones?'

'Shut up and you'll hear. Whoever created Rondua was fair. At all times, there are ten Bones of the Moon in existence. The five you found are called, collectively, The Bones of Smoke. The ones I found are called The Bones of Mark. Don't ask what the phrases mean, because I don't know. I do think they have something to do with the gods, or God, or whoever is in charge here. But that's only my opinion. Anyway, both sets of Bones are here and always have been. What happens in Rondua depends entirely on which set has been found.'

'Wait—'

'Stop interrupting me, Cullen. You won't have any questions when I'm finished, I can assure you. Both sets of Bones exist, but they must all be found by someone if they wish to gain power. A long time ago I found The Bones of Mark, so I've ruled Rondua since that time. You're familiar with my way of doing things, but I don't want to discuss policy with you because it would do no good. I rule the way I choose to rule.

'If you hadn't found The Bones of Smoke, Pepsi, I would have continued in power for another three Milans. Do you know how long a Milan is?'

Calm but attentive, Pepsi nodded.

'Good. Once someone finds the five Bones, either set, they rule for five Milans. Then they must take the test I'll describe to you in a little while.

'However, what you've done has thrown things off a bit. In the past, it has frequently happened that two have found the different sets of Bones at the same time, or almost the same time. Keegan Merle and Nile Shadows were the last ones to coincide. The law says that when that *does* happen, the test must be taken immediately by both, and only one will survive. That time, Merle won and ruled for his five Milans. Incidentally, Merle was Mr Tracy's father, in case you didn't know.

'After he was gone, there was a short period of no rule before I came along. I must tell you that I found the five Bones of Mark more quickly than anyone ever had in Rondua before.'

Looking pleased with himself, Chili reached over and picked up the fourth Bone of the Moon from the couch—the one that DeFazio had so indifferently given us when we went to his island; the one that looked like a baseball; the one I had used to save myself in another lifetime.

'What DeFazio said to you wasn't far from the truth, you know. Even *as* ruler of this place, you can create policy and institute some big changes, but unfortunately old ways and believers take a long time to die. No matter how clever or imaginative you are, you'll always be up against certain elements which stupidly refuse to go your way. For me, it's been idiots like Tracy and Stastny Panenka,

176

not to mention Sizzling Thumb who's as old as a rock and just as obtuse.

'The ways I've tried to persuade them! I've gone to them as Jack Chili, as Alvin Williams, as Fire Sandwich . . . you can't believe how I've tried to convince them to come over to my side!

'That's not to say, friend Pepsi, that even if you succeed today, you won't have exactly the same problems facing you tomorrow. Only your problem will be *my* followers who, I have to admit, are a dedicated lot.

'You'll have power. But short of killing everyone who disagrees with you—which you *could* do—you'll have to cajole and convince . . . All very boring, but part of the job.'

I found myself relaxing as Chili talked on, as if we were sitting with an old head of state who was reminiscing about his good old days in office. Except that this head of state was still in power and from the tone of his voice, expected to stay there.

'You find the Bones, become ruler and then, if no one else finds the other ones during your term, you are allowed to rule the way you want for five Milans. That's the history of Rondua in a few long sentences. As told by Jack Chili, Alvin Williams, Martio, Fire Sandwich, etcetera.'

'What happens at the end of those five Milans?'

'You take the test and die.'

There was silence for a long time—a silence which Chili used to watch both of us with an unreadable expression on his (on their?) face.

'Why is it called a test, then? Most tests you can either pass or fail.'

'Don't be obnoxious, Cullen. This isn't school; you don't go to history class next.' He had lapsed into Eliot's mimicking voice. 'I'm permitting you to stay here, so *don't* rub me the wrong way. It's called a test because that's what they call it, all right?'

My son was at stake and I had to say more. 'All right, but even if you succeed, you only live for five Milans? How long is that?'

'That's none of your business. You had your chance once, but Rondua is only a dream for you now. For us, it's life. Pepsi, you found the five Bones of Smoke, so now you have to take the test. And I must too.

'What you must also realize is that however "good" or "bad" you think you are, there's absolutely no telling who will win. There is no

177

sense to the way things are decided. I'm as frightened by this moment as you are.'

Bending forward, he opened both hands and two gigantic pistols appeared. They looked as big as shoe-boxes, beautifully black and oiled and sleek.

'Take one.'

Without hesitation, Pepsi chose one. It was too big for his small hand, so he had to hold it up with two.

'Wait!'

Chili's eyes flared and I sat back hard in my chair.

'We put them in our mouths like this.' He opened his mouth wide and slid the barrel in until the trigger loop rested on his bottom lip. Then he took it out again so that he could speak. 'You have every reason not to trust me, and I understand that, so I will go first. I'll pull the trigger and you will hear the explosion. But nothing will happen, no *decision* will be made until both of us have done it. That is the system and if I win, I continue to rule.'

My heart floated cold and dead in my chest. 'Pepsi. Pepsi, do you have to do this?'

'Yes, Mom. I have to. Mr Tracy said there would be something like this at the end; it's the only way things can work out.'

I turned to Chili. 'Can I have a minute? Can you give me some time? Some time alone with him?'

'Of course, Mrs James. Just don't have a fist-fight with him, like the clouds did.' The voice was perfect Alvin Williams. Getting up, Chili looked at my son and I knew they understood each other completely in a way I could never understand or be a part of. Chili walked out of the room; in the kitchen, I heard him at the sink drawing a glass of water.

I looked at my son as if I was drowning and in the instant before death, saw *our* life together flash through my mind. There was nothing I could say. But what did I *want* to say? Were there real words for love? Words heard that would mean something now, now when all was said and done and almost over?

Pepsi got off the couch, came to me and got down on his knees next to me. He put his head in my lap, his arms around my legs. I touched his hair as gently as I could and began to stroke it. It was so soft and thick—a little boy's hair—tangled and dreamily soft.

Death doesn't make you sad—it makes you empty. That's what's so bad about it. All of your charms and beliefs and funny habits fall

178

fast through a big black hole, and suddenly you know they're gone because just as suddenly, there's nothing at all left inside.

> Funny guys in funny ties,
> Wearing helmets, telling lies.
> Walk right here, your place is free.
> I love you and you love me.

The Song of the Wooden Mice. It was the only thing that came out of my new emptiness, but it was all right and I had enough voice to sing it quietly to my good son Pepsi.

Pressing his head deeper into my lap, he held my legs tightly, so goddamned tightly.

> Wooden mice know what's nice;
> Sawdust cheese and maple spice.

He was crying and I was his mother and that was all. The only time left to us was this moment.

'You are the best, Pepsi. Everything you've done has made me proud. I'll love you all my life. And if there's anything afterwards, I'll love you after I die too. Do you understand me?'

'Yes, Mom.'

Chili had come up behind us without making a sound. Now he belched loudly.

'Let's go.'

Pepsi started to get up, but he stumbled on my foot and fell against me.

'Get up! Stop messing around! Take the gun and let's go.' Chili's voice was much higher; it was someone else's voice, someone I didn't know. He was scared too.

They sat on either side of the couch and Chili put the pistol inside his mouth and waited. Pepsi tried to do the same thing, but the gun was way too big and he gagged trying to put it as far down his throat.

'Just put it *in* your mouth, Stupid! Don't waste my time!'

Pepsi closed his mouth and swallowed. Opening it again, he did what Chili ordered.

'As I said, I'll go first.'

179

There wasn't even time to look. The blast from Chili's gun filled the room completely.

I whipped my head his way as the second explosion came. I screamed, 'Pepsi!' just as my eyes found Jack Chili . . .

Who looked exactly the same as he had an instant before.

8

I was awake. I was home and I was awake. I was in my house and this was my real world. I knew too, instinctively, instantly, that I would never go back to Rondua, no matter what happened to my son. *That* was why Chili had allowed me to remain while he explained the test: he knew I would go away for ever.

I threw the covers off me and fled the room, the bed, everything. The apartment was pitch-black, street light my only guide. I ran for the living-room to see what was there, if Pepsi or Chili were there. But nothing was there. Then something . . .

'Oh!'

Eliot, who'd been spending nights on the couch since Danny had gone, shot up and looked wildly at me. 'What is it? What's wrong, Cullen?'

'Where's the baby? Where's Mae?'

'God, Cullen, what happened? What's wrong?'

'Where is the *baby?*'

'In bed, in her crib. Take it easy! What's the matter with you? What's wrong?'

I moved the last few steps to the crib and looked down for my other child, praying *she* would be there and all right. She was! Awake and looking very angrily at me.

Scooping her up, I held her to my hot chest. She began to cry, but that didn't matter. Nothing mattered but her being there, well and safe in my arms.

Holding her to me, I looked around the room. The couch held only scattered sheets and a blanket, a pillow crushed up against one of the arm-rests.

'Cullen, will you please tell me what the hell is going *on?*'

181

'I had a Rondua dream. I think Pepsi's dead there. I don't want to talk. Let me walk around and then I'll tell you.'

Eliot sat on the couch and watched me pace the room. He wore bright red flannel pyjamas and his hair stood up all over his head. I thought of when I had touched Pepsi's hair; it had only been a moment ago. I kept walking the room.

Some time later I looked at Mae and saw she'd gone back to sleep in my arms. I went to the crib and laid her carefully back there, covering her with the blanket Pepsi had so recently fingered. I watched Mae to make sure she existed, even in sleep.

I went to Eliot's chair on purpose and sat down. The chocolate stain was still there on the arm. All of my energy was gone.

'Do you want some coffee? Let me go make you some Decaf, Cullen.' Eliot was already half-way to the kitchen when he said it.

I listened to him rummaging around in there and thought of Jack Chili drinking water from the tap. Was his glass still in the sink?

'You don't have any Decaf left, Cullen. You want me to go and get some?'

'No, I'm all right.'

'Don't be silly. Wait here and I'll get some down at my place. I've got the blend you like, that I buy at "The Daily Grind". It'll only take me two secs to do it.'

At the door he turned and asked loudly if there was anything else I wanted. I didn't want anything; I wanted to know about my son. I heard Eliot unclicking the different locks on the door, heard him say he'd be back in two shakes.

The door hit the wall with a tremendous *Bang!* Looking up, I heard Eliot say, 'Hey!' and then throw his hands up against something which was going on outside in the hall.

Then there was another sound—the loudest, hardest *thud* I had ever heard.

Eliot made another noise, then fell straight backwards into the hallway. It was all too fast for me to register what was happening. I watched Eliot fall; saw the rainbow of blood from his head rise and follow him down, all the way down to the floor.

Someone knelt over him and smashed his head. One, two, three more times. Each sound was softer and wetter.

Then Alvin Williams got up and, quick as an animal, was in my apartment dragging Eliot in after him.

I finally understood what was happening. As I moved to my left,

182

for Mae, Williams saw me and shouted at me to stay still. He closed
the door behind him with his foot and I saw he was wearing brand-
new white sneakers.

He had what looked like a crowbar in his right hand. There was
blood and other coloured things all up and down it.

'Don't move! Don't do anything!'

He bent over Eliot and smashed the crowbar into the unmoving
body again. Straightening up, he slid one glistening hand down the
shaft of the bar and wiped what came off on his pants.

'Nanika nomimasho. That's Japanese! It means, "Do you want to
have a drink?" I know Japanese now. I studied!'

As he started into the room, I threw a hand out against him, as I
had with Weber Gregston and the gypsy. My arc of purple light flew
across the room, touched, landed low on the crowbar and sent a
green-gold bolt up and down it.

Williams watched as it lit up his hand. He laughed happily.
'Great!'

But the light did nothing else. There was only that light—no more
power behind it. I put out my other hand the same way. Again
nothing. Williams moved deeper into the room. The crowbar still
glowed.

'You didn't *write* me. You don't *like* me!'

I got up, lost my balance, fell back again. He watched.

'What do you want, Alvin?'

'What do I want? I want a letter! You've got to write me a letter!'

Furious now, he swung the crowbar out wildly to the side and hit
a standing lamp. It flew over and went out as soon as it hit the floor.
The room lost half of its light and the baby started screaming.

'A letter? Okay, let's do a letter. I'll write you a letter: "Dear
Alvin—"'

'Not *that* kind! A letter with stamps on it! From Japan. Arigato!
Send it to the shogun.'

'Okay, Alvin, let me get some paper. I've got some in the bedroom. Let's go in there.'

'Goddamn it, I want that letter. Why don't you have paper in
here?' Five feet away, he stepped towards the crib. I paralleled his
movement.

'Don't touch the baby. Just leave the baby alone, Chili! Don't
touch my baby!'

The name stopped him and he looked at me, confused. In desper-

183

ation, I threw my hand out at him again. It had worked once with Weber.

The arc came again, only this time slowly and lazily. It drifted in many colours across the room. Williams put up his hand, caught the light and put it in his mouth. He ate it.

He took two more steps towards the crib, looking at it now. I beat him there and stood with my back to it.

The crowbar still glowed. A light from inside Alvin's stomach glowed. My light. My magic. All gone.

'Hello, Mrs James. Remember me? Yours very sincerely, Alvin Williams.' He brought the flickering crowbar up over his head. He wanted me dead, so I threw myself on to the floor as far away from the baby as I could get. Maybe he would stop when I was dead.

A noise like a bomb shook the room and for an instant I thought I had already been hit, because at the same time a white light enveloped us all.

Williams spun around, his arms still high and cocked and ready.

The light was everywhere, but the sound was gone. Only white, full light and silence.

I heard something hit the ground with a hard *clang*. Alvin grunted once, then jerked sideways and fell near me. I saw what was left of his dead, split face. Something had hit in the middle of that face and everything had collapsed inwards.

'Mom?'

Pepsi stepped out of the white light and came to me. On my knees, I reached up for him but he shook his head. I wasn't allowed to touch him.

'You won, Pepsi!'

He nodded and smiled. 'Is that Mae, Mom? It is, isn't it?' His voice was his own, only hollower and much, much further away.

He went over to his sister and looked at her through the bars of her crib. I was on all fours when I watched my children meet for the first time.

Mae saw him and reached out her hand. She opened her mouth, closed it, smiled; she knew who he was, I'm sure of that.

'Hello, Mae.'

I closed my eyes. 'I love both of you. Mae sees you, Pepsi. I know she sees you. I love you both and you're both here now.'

He reached out a small finger and almost touched his sister's hand with it. 'Promise to always sing her the Mouse song, Mom.'

'I will.'

He pointed towards the window. New York City was gone and Mr Tracy's face filled the window instead. He smiled like old times.

'Always sing that one to her, Mom. And the one about the Spider Club too. That's a good one.'

The light grew in the room. It climbed from a swimming-pool blue, to orange, to yellow, higher yellow, white. It was too bright then and I had to close my eyes. When I opened them again, both Pepsi and Mr Tracy were gone.

When the police arrived, I had Mae in my arms and the crowbar across my wet lap. All of the blood had soaked through my cotton nightgown and on to my thighs. It didn't feel bad.

Alvin Williams had escaped two hours before. Doctor Lavery had completely forgotten about me in the initial confusion. When he did remember, he called the police right away. But they took a while to arrive.

Williams had hailed a cab, strangled the driver, stolen the man's money and the tire-iron from the trunk of the car.

Tire-iron. That's what the policeman called the thing. A tire-iron. Alvin still had the key to the front door of our building in his pocket. They said it had been his prized possession at the Institute, so they'd allowed him to keep it.

I wouldn't let the police take Mae or the tire-iron away from me. They took Eliot. Then they took Alvin. But I wouldn't let them take Mae or the tire-iron.

When they asked how I had gotten it away from Alvin, I shrugged and said *I* hadn't—Pepsi had.

They left me alone.

Danny buried Eliot, then moved us out of that apartment within nine days after it happened. We live on Riverside Drive now, and there is a little bit of a view of the Hudson River. Danny laughed and said he had to pay off three people to get that view, but he wanted me to have it.

In bed last night he held me again and said he wanted to talk to me for the rest of our lives. He wanted to wake up talking to me and go to bed talking. He said we would help each other grow old.

Do you know what I've been thinking about? Thinking about a lot? Whether Eliot is with Pepsi now. Even if he first had to go to

185

Ophir Zik, I know Pepsi would get Eliot out of there in a flash. That would be great. They would have so much fun together.

There's no way to express how much I miss them.

It's hard convincing yourself that where you are at the moment is your home, and it's not always where your heart is. Sometimes I win and sometimes not.